P9-CRB-792

Accidentally Fabulous

·

The fashion-forward
adventures of Imogene

Written by
Lisa Barham

Illustrated by
Sujean Rim

SIMON PULSE
New York   London   Toronto   Sydney

Accidentally Fabulous

The fashion-forward adventures of Imogene

For Jack

This book is a work of fiction. Any references to historical events, real
people, or real locales are used fictitiously. Other names, characters,
places, and incidents are the product of the author's imagination,
and any resemblance to actual events or locales or persons, living
or dead, is entirely coincidental.

SIMON PULSE ✳ An imprint of Simon & Schuster Children's
Publishing Division ✳ 1230 Avenue of the Americas, New York, NY
10020 ✳ Copyright © 2008 by Lisa Barham ✳ All rights reserved,
including the right of reproduction in whole or in part in any form. ✳
SIMON PULSE and colophon are registered trademarks of Simon &
Schuster, Inc. ✳ Designed by Karin Paprocki ✳ The text of this book
was set in Cochin. ✳ Manufactured in the United States of America
✳ First Simon Pulse edition August 2008 ✳ 10 9 8 7 6 5 4 3 2 1
✳ Library of Congress Control Number 2008921518
ISBN-13: 978-1-4169-1445-7 ✳ ISBN-10: 1-4169-1445-5

acknowledgments

It is with great appreciation that I thank the following: my friends Claudia Hilbert and Frank Spina; my agent, Jodi Reamer; Caroline Abbey; Anica Rissi, Bethany Buck, and Karin Paprocki at Simon & Schuster; and Sujean Rim, who somehow always manages to magically capture the soul of Imogene. Above all, I would like to thank my husband, Tom, for his meticulous eye and unwavering support, and my son, Jack . . . just because.

Hollywood Rule Number One:

ALWAYS BE THE STAR
OF YOUR OWN MOVIE.

A Long Time Ago in a Galaxy Far, Far Away . . .

date: LATE WINTER

mood: ILLUMINATED

❋   ❋   ❋

I n case you haven't noticed, the celeb thing is totally rampant. I mean, *everyone* wants to be one. Everyone except me, that is — or so I thought. I never wanted to be a celebrity. I just wanted to be a star.

It all began one warm summer night. As I reached out to open my bedroom window, something caught my eye. Nestled on a blanket of black velvet sky was a star, glittering like some flawless five-billion-carat Cartier diamond. It was so much more brilliant than all the others that I simply couldn't take my eyes off of it.

From that night on I'd climb into my bed and gaze out at the sky as my little star put on its nightly show, twinkling away just for me. I loved it so much, I vowed to be just like it when I grew up: beautiful, radiant, a shimmering light more dazzling than all those around it. But then one evening as I tucked the covers under my chin, the unthinkable happened — my star had disappeared. For weeks I searched the sky for my shining companion, but to no avail. At first I was heartbroken; it felt as if I'd lost my best friend. But strangely, even though my star was no longer visible, I could still feel its presence, silently guiding me through all the events in my life. That star held my destiny.

I never shared that belief with anyone. Not even Evie, who knows just about everything there is to know about me — *and then some.* You see, in my heart of hearts I knew that one day my star would reappear; that fate would come calling, and when it did, something glorious would happen. Though truth be known, I never thought it would happen quite so soon.

chapter one

L.A. Dolce Vita

Journal Check:

• *Evie and I arrive at LAX airport and obtain cool rental car.*
(Pulling up to The Ivy in a Hummer H2
would be completely diabolical.)

• *Exit airport. Get nearly run off the road*
by an army of rogue Priuses.

• *Pick up star maps from roadside stand.*

• *Scout L.A. trends, then onward to our spring break destination:*
Fashion Fantasy Camp!

❋ ❋ ❋

A searing blast of hot desert wind hit me as I twirled out of Barneys' revolving door into the glaring Southern California sunlight. Toy dropped his stuffed animal (Boo Boo II) and panted. Evie had Toy's water bottle, and I was getting a bit concerned. Maybe the "divide and conquer" approach to our fashion scouting mission had been a mistake. I flipped down my sunglasses and frantically slurped the remaining icy morsels of a Starbucks macchiato in an attempt to stave off *Spontaneous Dehydration Syndrome*—a mummylike malady peculiar to West Coast dwellers, where just crossing the sidewalk could prove fatal to one's skin tone.

It was two fifteen, and Evie was late. Toy glanced up at me and sighed. I had to get him some water soon. There was a deli across the street, but with my luck Evie would show up as soon as I went inside. Though I really had no choice.

No sooner had I stepped off the curb than a red Mini Cooper convertible careened down Wilshire Boulevard. The car jerked into a sudden U-turn and screeched wildly across two lanes of oncoming traffic, nearly causing a multicar pileup. It skidded to a halt scarcely an inch in front of me. I scanned Toy and myself. Thankfully we were still alive and undamaged.

"Yo, moron!" someone shouted from a passing car. "Where do you think you are? New York?"

I cringed with secondhand embarrassment. To say that Evie's driving skills were unappreciated by the locals would be an understatement. Unfortunately, there was nothing I could do about it. We'd made a pact to share the driving and today was her day.

"Girlena!" Evie cried, oblivious to the grumbling onlookers who were forcibly detoured around her illegally parked car.

She waved a brand-new Malibu Barbie over her head. "Barbie says get in the car!"

We may have outgrown Santa Claus and the Easter Bunny, but Evie and I still secretly believe in Barbie. Well, Evie does anyway.

Evie cleared the candy wrappers and star maps off the front seat as I loaded my shopping bags. No trip to L.A. would be complete without shopping, and I'd charged a few trendy samples to my Hautelaw expense account. (More on that later.) The rule of thumb in trends is, the minute you know about a trend, it's as good as over. Even before a single stitch of clothing is sold, we fashion forecasters are two years down the road onto the next phase. I mean, *What's next* is preprogrammed into our DNA.

Without further ado, I scooped up Toy and clambered into the car. Having found his bottle underneath my seat, I poured said water into an empty Pinkberry frozen yogurt dish. Toy slurped gratefully, and I buckled the two of us in. Evie hit the gas and my eyes rolled heavenward. I prayed I'd told my parents I loved them before I left. I mean, whenever Evie was behind the wheel of anything beyond a tricycle, my thoughts invariably turned to life's tenuous nature—how one should always strive to live every day as if it were one's last.

I shouldn't complain though. Were it not for Evie, I'd be spending spring break home in Greenwich, slogging through the dreary late winter slush, passing my days watching reruns of *The Hills*, and hosting my own private pity party over the MIA status of my boyfriend. Paolo would be physically unavailable no matter where in the world I spent spring break, due to the fact that he'd be studying for midterms over the next two weeks. Talk about frustrating!

I felt like I was going through some weird mid-teen-life crisis or something. I mean, out of the blue, questions had begun to bubble up from my subconscious. Questions like: Does Paolo really love me? Will our relationship last forever? Why are sample sales always on Mondays? Should I get a goldfish? And it was getting worse by the day. Evie said that if I didn't do something about it, I'd be in danger of losing my glitter, not to mention my sparkle, shimmer, and shine.

"It's time to recapture your *la dolce vita*, girlfriend," she announced one night while devouring a croque monsieur at Meli-Melo. "You know," she said, munching, "get your joie de vivre back . . . reconnect with your inner self."

I figured she was onto something, because as she continued her analytical exploration of my psyche, I noticed that I'd cut my crepe up into a series of little frowny faces and scattered them around my plate.

"Worry not, dearest girlena." Whenever she says *that*, I know I'm doomed. "I have just the cure."

That's when she sprang it on me. Her dad was opening a

new restaurant in L.A., and he had scored two of the hottest (according to Evie) spring break tickets in the fashion universe: Fashion Fantasy Camp, an exclusive new venture started by one of his patrons.

Whatever Fashion Fantasy Camp was, it contained my two favorite words: *fashion* and *fantasy*. And far be it for me to squander a potentially life-altering experience. I mean, if there's one thing I'm not, it's a squanderer, though Lord knows I come from a long line of them.

The more I thought about it, the more I realized that Evie was right—this could be just the thing to snap me out of my funk. Not to mention reinforce my reputation as *the* fashion-forward go-to girl-about-town. (A moment of clarification: In addition to writing a fashion column, "Daily Obsession," for my school newspaper, I, Imogene, also intern at Hautelaw—the *glammiest* fashion forecasting company in the world.) I mean, in Greenwich—where the trick-or-treaters accept credit cards on Halloween—exclusive, firsthand experience is compulsory! Plus, Fashion Fantasy Camp would provide two weeks of best-friend bonding time in the land of gorgeous beaches, trendy spa treatments, fabulous nightlife, and nonstop celebs. So you see, I just *had* to say yes.

So where was I? Oh yes, zooming down Wilshire Boulevard on our way to the obligatory stop at Pink's (Evie's nothing if not a fast-food worshipper).

While Evie ordered our Lord of the Rings onion rings and Star Wars Dogs, my phone vibrated an incoming text message.

"Please be interesting," I prayed to the iPhone gods. To my complete euphoria, it was Paolo, the one and only love of my life. I mean, don't get me wrong, I've had crushes (I refer specifically to my long-held infatuation with Orlando Bloom), but the minute I laid eyes on Paolo, that was it. Gone! Of course, it didn't hurt that he is totally sexy and totally Italian, and made gangly ol' me feel totally beautiful from the very first moment we met. Yes, I know that sounds like some cheesy old movie, or some trite romance novel, but that's exactly what made it so special. I mean, I was definitely not the type of person who believed in love at first sight. But the rules that make up the game of love are full of exceptions, and in my case, Paolo was definitely the exception.

> **PGlam (as in Paolo Glamonti):**
> **Greetings from NYC, mi amore!**
> **Have u been discovered yet?**
> **Hautelawgirl: Lol! That's your job.**
> **You're the 1 studying to b a**
> **filmmaker—my life is fashion,**
> **remember?**
> **PGlam: You never know.** ☺
> **Hautelawgirl: Ha-ha. Like that wld**
> **ever hapn.**
> **PGlam: Just don't 4get the little**
> **people when yr on top. And while**
> **you're out there, shld u happen to**
> **run into any agents, pls give them**
> **my#.**

Hautelawgirl: I'll certainly keep my eyes peeled for 1 on my next trip to Spago. (As if!)

PGlam: Miss u amore . . .

The remaining text message has been deliberately censored. Sorry to omit the juicy bits, but I draw the line at e-kissing and telling.

When we finished our last bite, Evie climbed behind the wheel again, to the usual bleating horns and screeching tires as we sped west on Sunset Boulevard at Mach 2.

Not that I was paying attention or anything—by then I was far too busy gaping at movie billboards as they sailed past. And from the way the car kept swerving out of its lane, I could tell Evie was enraptured by the billboards too. Between the two of us, she'd always been the more starstruck, predicating her numerous collections on old film stars. From Rita Hayworth, a little cocktail number shot with Chantilly lace; the Audrey Hepburn, a black halter column à la *Breakfast at Tiffany's* (my personal fave); the Sophia Loren—think black lace Sicilian widow; and the Grace Kelly, a fitted bodice with fluffy layers of embroidered ballerina chiffon at the skirt à la *Rear Window*. The obsession is endless. And so is Evie's talent.

As for *moi*, I've known from birth that I wanted to be something huge in the fashion world. My original vision of my future went way beyond Coco Chanel worship. My ambition was to become the huge fashion goddess that I knew was lurking deep down in my soul. Poor Mom and

9

Dad. I think they thought they had a real nutcase on their hands. I mean, at age three, while everyone else was making mud pies, I was reupholstering my doll furniture with collage cutouts from *Vogue*. By the time I'd reached third grade I had my first Chanel bag—I traded Tessa Henson my mom's Martha Stewart garden set for her mom's pink and black double-C *pochette*. (I was a shrewd negotiator.) When I was ten, I asked for a fully let-out sable coat—I didn't get one. Growing up with friends from some of the wealthiest families in the country, I was the poorest little rich girl in Greenwich. Raised in a gardener's cottage, I spent my days as the local poster child for the underprivileged, living on hope and falling regularly into the sanctuary of my own imagination (okay, so I'm into escapism, huge!), daydreaming endlessly about my future at the top of the fashion heap. But with the aforementioned onslaught of my little pre–spring break *crise de faith*, I suddenly felt uncertain as to which way to go. I began to wonder if there was something even bigger out there waiting for me—some *grand, defining purpose*. And I guess, somewhere in the back of my mind, I was secretly hoping that this trip would reveal it and restore my, as Evie put it, *la dolce vita*. And that when spring break was over, I'd return home a bright, shiny new me.

I glanced over at Evie.

A faint smile crossed her lips when I said her name. While I was off lost in my own thoughts, she had clearly been doing a bit of musing of her own.

I nudged Evie gently to assure myself that her mind was still intact. Then, as if she'd just untangled the meaning of life she announced, "I've got it!"

Got what? Did I miss something? "Maybe we should pull over," I said.

"I can't believe it never occurred to me!"

"What?"

"Picture it, girlena . . . me—a costume designer. I mean, everyone knows that Seventh Avenue is so twentieth century."

"Do they?"

"*Really!*" she whined, noting my one arched eyebrow. "You *know* I adore all things Hollywood, right? Well, combine that with my love of fashion design. Don't you see? What could be more natural?"

It actually did sound logical. Costume design was the perfect future for Evie, and L.A. was the perfect place to do it. And with the palm trees, movie billboards, Bentleys, and an eternal summer, I could see how easily someone could get wrapped up in the idea of her very own, up-close-and-personal fifteen minutes here.

Evie, still reeling from her "Eureka!" moment, placed two connected Twizzlers between her teeth, tore off one, and handed the other to me.

"A celebratory snack," she announced, giggling, "and a

toast to our future. Who knows, Fashion Fantasy Camp might very well turn into Fashion Reality Camp!"

A smile finally sprang to my lips. "Here's to Tinseltown . . . I guess."

We slapped our Twizzlers together, beamed each other our best BFF smiles, and chewed off into the sunset.

chapter two

The Devil Wears Dolce

date: MARCH 12
to: MES CHÉRIES
from: MOI, IMOGENE
re: HOT FASHION FLASH!
DRESSES ARE THE NEW
PETS.

Case in point: While roaming through Fred Segal in my unquenchable search for the new, I experienced a totally strange phenomenon when I came upon a just-about-to-go-on-sale dress. It literally looked so forlorn and rejected, I swear it cried out to me, "Please take me home with you and love me." So I did.

✳   ✳   ✳

The scent of sunscreen, a back note of Eau de Pacific Ocean and a hint of Chanel No. 90210 engulfed us as we stepped onto the sand. Our hotel, Shutters on the Beach, was literally *on the beach*. And our camp orientation was too.

No sooner had I tapped out my obligatory "Daily Obsession" e-mail blast when a deeply burnished woman air-kissed her way toward the enormous cabana-like structure in front of the growing crowd. From its edge flew a banner that read WELCOME TO FASHION FANTASY CAMP!

The woman held a clipboard in one hand and a bullhorn in the other. That's where her mouth was.

"All right, people! Let's get this moving!"

On tiptoe I lurched forward, craning my neck above a cluster of campers circulating in front of me. Fashion tribes of every ilk filled the beach. To our left: eighties girls swathed in early Madonna; to our right: California girls clad in recycled denim miniskirts. And in the "fashion hurts" category stood one lone guy in leggings, looking a tad like fashion roadkill. (Although I will say his Gucci man-purse totally outfoxed mine.) As for me, I wore a simple pair of vintage Chantal Thomas shorts and a top à la Evie. Thankfully, as far as fashion goes, I have a fairy god-BFF. For years Evie's been sewing up renditions of chic designer pieces, which we also sell to our GCA (Greenwich Country Academy) classmates at deeply discounted rates.

As I scanned the beach, I began feeling a bit intimidated. You'd think that by the age of seventeen, self-esteem would no longer be an issue. But with all the peer pressure and personal insecurities I'd endured since my preteen years, I was still a bit nervous about how I'd fit in. By the look of it, I wasn't alone. Everyone around me was stealing not-so-subtle peeks at their new campmates, mentally crunching in-depth mathematical equations intended to calculate the pecking order they fell into.

While I continued scanning the crowd in the hopes of absorbing good energy from those I perceived to be New Yorkers, Evie was devouring the handout someone had shoved at her on our way in.

"Listen to this," she said, sweeping her long, silky bangs to one side. "'Share the limelight with living legends. Fashion Fantasy Camp is a one-of-a-kind experience that brings fashion lovers together with professionals for an unforgettable opportunity to move from mere spectator to fashion star.'"

She grabbed my hand and squeezed it tightly. "Girlena, this is going to be our best spring break ever!" I squeezed back.

The bullhorn woman had climbed onto a beach chair and was now in full view of the crowd.

"Welcome, Fashion Fantasy Campers." Her voice quavered as the chair wobbled in the sand. She steadied herself and swept away a few windblown strands of hair, which grazed her silicone-enhanced cheekbones.

"For those who don't already know me, I'm Cory, your head counselor, and I want to welcome you all to our first-ever Fashion Fantasy Camp!"

The crowd applauded with uncertainty.

15

"We are about to open the sign-in tables, so listen carefully, people. Those of you whose surnames begin with the letters A through M, line up with Brandy." She gestured like someone directing a jumbo jet on the tarmac at JFK.

"Brandy, raise your hand so people can see you!"

Brandy, a diminutive woman with straight blond hair, stuck her hand in the air. She and her cadre of cohorts were dressed à la O.C.-wear: deep décolleté blouses, tight-fitting miniskirts, and high, high, cork-wedged sandals.

"N through Z, line up with Brianna over there!"

"Come on." I grabbed Evie and pushed my way through a gaggle of Havaianas-clad flip-floppers. "We're somewhere over there."

"Once you sign in," Cory continued, "you'll receive a check-in packet containing your schedule for the next two weeks. Then you'll go through the pool deck over there and cross the hall to the east wing for our opening presentation. After which you will be sorted into teams, or "Fashion Houses"—she made quotation marks with her fingers—"as we like to call them, and learn all the details of your first fashion assignment."

"Ooh, it sounds a bit Harry Potter, doesn't it, girlena?" Evie said excitedly. "I wonder where they keep the Sorting Hat?"

After a grueling fifteen minutes on line, Evie and I found ourselves standing before a woman with a pink HELLO: MY NAME IS CHRISSY fake-fur-trimmed name tag stuck to her sundress. Chrissy took my registration card and studied me for several seconds, as if I were an alien from planet Inappropriately Dressed. Had I known I was going to be standing on the beach, I guess I would have broken out my gold lamé Kamali swimsuit.

Chrissy glanced at Toy and smiled. "Dogs are our alter egos, aren't they?" she said, admiring his outfit. Evie had refashioned a wisp of tulle for his collar, which faintly resembled fairy wings.

Chrissy mindlessly pet her name tag and traced her matching pink fake-fur-tipped pen up and down the rows of her spreadsheet, presumably in search of my name.

"Now, let's just make sure this is filled out properly, shall we? Name: Imogene. Hometown: Greenwich, Connecticut. Age: Seventeen. Occupation: Student-slash-fashion-forecasting-intern-slash-*culturepreneur*." She ogled me for a few seconds. "Excuse me for staring, but aren't you that Hautelaw Girl?"

"She is," Evie confirmed.

Okay. Time to press the rewind button.

A few words about Hautelaw Girl and my alleged semi-celebrity status: Remember the part where I'm an intern at Hautelaw? Well, I also have a little video blog. (Didn't you know? Blog is the new black.) It all started last summer, when I managed to talk my boss into sending me to Paris for Couture Week, which is where my video blog made its debut. After all, one's daily adventures deserve an equally fashionable delivery, *n'est-ce pas*? The role of *moi*, aka Hautelaw Girl, my default sobriquet, was played by *moi*, of course. Anyway, under normal circumstances, a trip to Paris would have been a dream come true. I mean, think

17

about it: the fashion, the romance, the petit fours, the steady stream of Ladurée macaroons . . . *Ooh!* But I digress. As with so many best-laid plans, this one didn't exactly work out the way it was supposed to. In fact it was nearly a disaster, but that's another story. I did, how-

ever, manage to get the inside scoop on the Yves Montrachet couture collection, replete with exclusive interviews, feedback from fashion insiders at the show, and gobs of juicy gossip—reported only with the strictest interest in complete and honest journalism in mind. Following that, everything sort of took off. My video diaries became popular in their own right and attracted a modest following. *Ah, the power of the press . . .*

Okay, fast-forward to the present.

"I honestly didn't think you were a real person!" Chrissy gushed.

Since no one I'd encountered thus far in L.A. appeared to be real, this seemed like a fair statement. "With Coco Chanel as my witness," I replied, "every last molecule of me is real."

It was obvious that Chrissy was impressed with me, which naturally impressed me with her. She tilted her head sideways, as if formulating an entirely new thought, and pressed the pen to her lips. "You know, writing, fashion, and Hollywood are a powerful combination these days. Do you have an agent yet?"

"Agent?" I stared blankly, unsure what she meant or where she was going with this. "Not that I know of," I replied.

"I'm shocked! With all the adventures you've had, and your trip to Paris, and your video blog, and your fashion column . . . You know, I have this friend who has a friend whose hairdresser does Sheila Hicks. Maybe I can pass her your number."

"Sheila Hicks?" I repeated. The name didn't ring a bell.

"You really aren't from around here, huh?" She smiled. "Sheila just happens to be *the* Hollywood agent."

"You mean, as in movies?" Evie broke in.

"Movies, television, merchandising—you name it."

I shrugged off the possibility. Sure I'd love to have a major motion picture project about *moi* in the works, but at what cost? To have every sordid detail of my life story paraded in front of the public like some cheap vaudeville act? To be chased endlessly across the globe by hordes of crazed paparazzi? To have money, cars, A-list invites, designer clothes, and jewels thrust at me from the chicest corners of the universe?

"Are you staying here, at the hotel?"

"I'm in room 804."

As soon as Evie and I stepped inside the huge, gilded conference room, the chandeliers began flickering, indicating that the presentation was about to begin. Everyone scrambled to find a seat at one of the dozens of round tables placed throughout the large room. The presentation turned out to be a short history of fashion from togas to Tom Ford, ending in modern-day hyperbranding practices and mega-merchandising. Evie took copious notes. When the presentation finally ended, Cory came out on stage to a round of applause.

"All right!" she shouted into the microphone. "It's time to meet the esteemed industry experts who will be your fashion advisors!"

The room trembled with anticipation. After an appropriate dramatic pause, Cory cleared her throat and continued.

"Our talented faculty will serve as mentors through the many fashion projects that lay ahead over the next two weeks. You will team up with a partner and work to earn points through the completion of creative tasks and challenges. You and your partner will then apply your knowledge and skills toward finishing a project for our *final competition*, which will determine the best team at FFC, and"—another dramatic pause here—"a ten-thousand-dollar college scholarship sponsored by the CFDA (Council of Fashion Designers of America)!"

Everyone in the room reeled in elation. I, however, was still stuck on Cory's words, *"completing tasks . . . finishing projects . . . completing tasks . . . finishing projects . . ."*

A little-known fact re: *moi* is that, like Leonardo da Vinci, I've almost never finished anything I've started. Witness my life, littered with gobs of unfinished endeavors: half-knit sweaters, scraps of poems, incomplete home decor projects. I've tried *everything*, from piano lessons to snowboarding lessons to pottery lessons, all of which I dropped after about a nanosecond. The word "finish" freaks me out.

Evie, on the other hand, was totally exhilarated.

"Girlena, this is going to be greater than I thought! We've got this wrapped. You and I are the best team on earth!"

Cory began introducing the faculty lineup, while I, in the throes of regretting having come here in the first place, teetered on the edge of my seat, straining to hear over the din of applause as each successive superstar strolled out on the stage and took a bow. That's when Evie's FFC flyer slipped off the edge of the table. It landed facedown near my shoe. As I reached down to retrieve it, something on the back of it caught my eye. I fixed on the guest faculty head shots. It's too bad camouflage is currently out of style, because unexpectedly, all I wanted to do was disappear.

I don't remember much after that other than an overwhelming feeling of wooziness. Everything was mixed up. As I returned my body to its original upright position, my eyes involuntarily darted back and forth between the stage and the photo. My head sent a signal to my inner core, and pressed hard when it located my "completely insecure" button. I flashed back to my first meeting with *her*. When *she* was on the fast track to rising to the top of Hautelaw, when *she* was my boss—and my nemesis, having me running to Starbucks every hour on the hour, me zipping though the streets of NYC in search of that certain new bag that had a waiting list of a millennium, because she needed it by five p.m. I hadn't expected at the end of the summer to be made a senior intern and contributing editor. And I didn't mean to take her job. After all, she stole my ideas and sold them to our competition, then tried to steal Paolo, too. Spring had no choice but to fire her. She wound up at Haute & About, Hautelaw's cross-town rival headed by Winter Tan — Spring's sworn enemy.

I thought I was rid of her forever, but here she was now, center stage at Fashion Fantasy Camp, clad in the wickedest Dolce & Gabbana outfit I'd ever laid eyes on, while the entire audience applauded her in welcome.

Evie gasped in stunned horror as she faced me, her face veiled in sympathy.

"Imogene," she said.

I didn't react. I *couldn't*. Shock had already paralyzed my body.

"Imogene," Evie tried once more. "That's . . . it's . . ."

I prayed she wouldn't say that awful word — the *B* word. The word I can't bring myself to endure, let alone say aloud.

But it was too late. . . .

"It's Brooke!" she said.

chapter three

California Dreaming

d a t e : MARCH 12, 10:00 P.M.

m o o d : INCOMPLETE

❊   ❊   ❊

t was a long day's journey into night, and by ten p.m. I
was beyond knackered. After a too-short phone call from
Paolo and a quiet walk on the beach to clear my head of
Brooke, not to mention the concern I had for my imminent
Fashion Fantasy Camp responsibilities, I left Evie to her
own devices and fell into a deep sleep. I dreamt I was back
at Barneys, gazing at a wintry window display. And then
somehow I was suddenly *inside* the display window, skiing
down an Alpine mountain. And I was good. *Really* good . . .

"Chic ahoy!" a voice calls to me from behind.

I glance back over my shoulder to find the editor in

chief of *Harper's Bazaar* paraskiing toward me.

"Ohmigod! It *IS* you!" she gasps, touching down with a great *SWOOSH*. "We'd just *looovve* to have you guest edit our magazine! Of course, you'll be paid in the latest couture! Interested?"

"I'll think about it," I reply, deftly slicing over the frozen crest of the mountain. "I like to keep my options open."

"Here's my private number," she cries, handing me her card at sixty miles an hour. "Call me anytime—day or night!"

And with that her paraskis lift off and she's gone. I hard cut right, then left, nearly clipping a couple walking their white snow leopard across the mountainous landscape.

I check my lip gloss before jumping a deep cornice with ease, lithely careening down the fresh-powder, double-black-diamond slalom course where, as it so happens, the Winter Olympics are under way. Hunky snowboarders stop cold and gape in awe as I speed past—the auburn highlights of my windblown hair sparkling in the winter sunlight, delicately framing my freckly, rosy cheekbones.

Abruptly I catch an edge and lose a ski in deep powder. I have to finish the run on one leg. But there's a glitch. Snow begins falling heavily, and the most difficult part of the run lies ahead: a sheer, forty-five-degree line down the mountain. No worries. I lock my sights on the herd of gaga men gathered at the finish line, their eyes riveted on the heavenly vision of *moi* floating down the slope like a Lanvin ski angel. A hottie from the Italian snowboarding team swerves alongside, flashing a brilliant smile.

"The Olympic Committee wants you to have this," he

says in a deep, sexy voice, and sticks an official Olympics emblem on my jacket.

"Really?!" I reply, beyond excited.

"Yes, really. By the way, do you believe in love at first sight?"

"Doesn't everyone?" I smile, radiating my natural je ne sais quoi. My pulse races with giddy anticipation as he invites me back to his multi-zillion-dollar chalet, après-ski.

Then suddenly, in a blaze of star-studded nebulae, he kisses me—so expertly that my Guerlain Kiss Kiss lip gloss remains perfectly intact. We kiss, and kiss, and kiss, with the crowd going berserk as I near the finish line. Unfortunately, I'm so busy kissing that I unknowingly veer onto another trail, missing the finish line by a mile. I shove the Italian stallion aside in a desperate attempt to get back on the right path, but it's too late. Another skier is already in the winner's circle, surrounded by adoring fans, draped in the gold medal—*my* gold medal!

chapter four

Rules of Engagement

date: MARCH 13

aries: ENCOUNTERS WITH SCINTILLATING PEOPLE ARE FORECAST FOR TODAY. THE CURRENT COSMIC CLIMATE MEANS THAT EVERYONE WANTS TO BE YOUR SPECIAL FRIEND, SO BE OPEN AND INVITING AND RECEPTIVE AND YOUR DATEBOOK WILL SOON BE FULL.

woke up bright and early, feeling refreshed. Evie was still asleep, so I headed for the pool deck, where breakfast awaited.

"Niiice!" the waiter exclaimed, ogling my ensemble. "You must be from New York or something. I can *always* tell."

Despite the fact that it was nearly ninety degrees, I was dressed—thank you, GCA thrift shop—to the nines in Chanel. I mean, if you could rewind my life, beginning with the day I took my holy vows, "lenahC ot efil ym etoved htrofecneh I," you would totally understand what makes me tick. Besides, you never know whom you might run into poolside at one's cute and *très* adorable hotel. This is Hollywood, after all—a place where just sitting innocently with your morning double-shot latte could bring a bolt of fame from out of the blue. Actually, it was two double espressos, and a plate of caramelized French toast, followed by equal measures of blogging, texting Paolo, journaling, e-mail blasting my latest installment of the "Daily Obsession," and reading a week's worth of *Variety*. Who would have guessed that the number of films and TV shows in production in New York this month was 125?

I had just decided that it was time to drag Evie out of bed by her hair, when the waiter returned with an herbal smoothie (a complimentary chaser from the chef) and Evie.

Without a word, she placed a small white box down on the table. Dangling from its elaborate lilac ribbon hung a small card with my name on it. Inside, an elegant, hand-engraved invitation encircled a French hyacinth-scented candle. Even though I'd been expecting it, my hand trembled slightly as I opened the box. It must have cost the earth. Though when you're marrying a *gazillionaire*, not to mention the world's most eligible bachelor, *that* hardly mattered.

I slurped my smoothie and read:

MRS. CORDELIA SAN JUAN MIGUEL

DE AUGUST-REYNARD

OF

PARIS, MADRID, NEW YORK, AND BUENOS AIRES

CORDIALLY INVITES YOU TO CELEBRATE THE

ENGAGEMENT OF

CAPRICE

AND

EDUARD SAN JUAN DE MIGUEL AUGUST-REYNARD

WEDNESDAY, MARCH 7

SIX O'CLOCK P.M.

THE SPA, BEVERLY HILLS HOTEL

(DRESS TO IMPRESS)

A beauty junkie bar none, only Caprice would come up with the genius idea of having her wedding shower at her favorite L.A. day spa. What had previously been only a theory would soon become a reality. I have to admit, when Caprice first called me to break the news of her engagement, I didn't believe she would actually go through with it. Even seeing the announcement on the first page of the *New York Times* Weddings and Celebrations section didn't make it seem real, especially since the *New York Times* no longer publishes engagement notices. I guess when you're a supermodel who's going to tie the knot with Eduard August-Reynard, the newly minted EAR-Media-conglomerate-CEO-slash-heir to a multi-billion-dollar family fortune, the *Times* makes an exception.

Even with all that going for him, somewhere in the back of my mind I still figured it was just another one of Caprice's *caprices*. Like when she was secretly engaged to the scion of Italian automaker Ferrari. Or when she pretended to elope with Leonardo DiCaprio, creating a humongous media frenzy that lasted for months. (I still see snippets of it in tabloids at the supermarket checkout.) Not too shabby for a nineteen-year-old from the Bronx via Puerto Rico.

Anyway, Caprice, with all her relatively newfound fashion fame, has bigger plans than spending the rest of her days as a career mannequin. Much bigger. In January she headed for L.A. to pursue acting, plunging headfirst into a plethora of casting calls with all the force of Hurricane Camille.

As it turned out, one of EAR Media's holdings just happened to be the successful Panoply Productions, which meant that Caprice had, at the very least, a fighting chance of landing *something* on camera. It's not that Caprice couldn't do it without Eduard's help—she could. The prevailing sentiment, however, was why expend all that energy if you didn't have to? I wondered what it would be like to be as gifted in the beauty department as Caprice. Not that I'm jealous of her or anything. I wish her the best in everything she does. But some people just walk out their front door and success falls on their head. Sure, she's paid her dues and everything. But this got me wondering: What is she doing that I'm *not* doing? How come it's so crystal clear for some people?

W e arrived at the spa a bit early after a long first day at Fashion Fantasy Camp, where we sat through a quickie lecture on *"Sleeves in Fashion: Dropped, Dolman, or Cut In? Is your armhole spot on or way out?"*, then attended a workshop on *"It-Bag 101: Clutch, Tote, Hobo, or Minaudiere. From Balenciaga to Goyard, What Every Girl Needs to Know,"* successfully avoiding any run-ins or encounters with the dreaded Brooke (who, thank Chanel, was nowhere in sight) and received our first assignment: a fashion treasure hunt called "Mission Impeccable." We were given twenty-four hours to find the following items:

- **one Pucci peignoir, lavender or green** (circa 1968)
- **one Jacques Fath draped chiffon cocktail dress** (61 extra points for yellow)
- **one Norma Kamali c. 1984 draped white jersey gown** (48 extra points if it has a coordinating hat)
- **one pair of Maud Frizon cone heels** (any color)

The team that brought in the most items from the list would win the event. Which had something to do with, not that I was paying attention, the *ultimate* challenge.

Evie and I waded through the pastel, flower-laden reception area of the spa, where guests were already sipping Kir Royales and nibbling personalized wedding-cake-shaped cookies with Caprice and Eduard's monograms piped in triple buttercream frosting.

I spotted Caprice chatting wistfully around a smattering of tables where multiple manis were already under way. All talk in the room seemed to be about the impending nuptials in Bali. Apparently the *do* would boast four hundred carefully cultivated guests and a private performance by Andrea Bocelli. Ordinarily all this would have thrilled Caprice—or anyone else for that matter—to no end, but instead of looking elated, Caprice seemed to be pushing back a frown.

My spider-sense kicked in, and I managed to hustle her into a private massage room for a much-needed girlo-a-girlo chat. But not before glomming a tube of Bain de Soleil bronzer on the way, for a much-needed Côte d'Azur (via L.A.) new look.

As we slathered it on, I plied her with questions about her expeditious wedding plans and waited for her to crack.

"I don't know." Caprice sighed, collapsing into a fluffy pile of fresh towels. "It's just that I don't want to let anyone down. Especially my mom."

"What does she have to do with this?"

"Are you kidding? She has everything to do with this. Mom's had a subscription to *Martha Stewart Weddings* since I was a girl. Even though marriage has never been my first priority . . . or my second, or my last, by any stretch of the imagination. I'm only nineteen, for Lord's sake. I am not ready for joint checking accounts, fertility, or becoming anyone's happy little homemaker."

As if that would ever happen.

I shook my head. "I don't get it."

"You're not supposed to. I'm not even sure I do. It's complicated."

"Try me," I said, leaning closer.

"Where I come from, you're supposed to graduate high school, get married, have a big family—the bigger the better. And that's about it. I mean, I have seven brothers and four sisters, and my aunt has five daughters and three sons. My sister Caroline, who is only two years older than me, just had her third baby! What you see in there," she said waving a freshly bronzed hand, "is nothing. I don't even know how many people there are in my extended family. Probably hundreds, thousands!"

"And you're going to carry on the tradition."

"*Mira*, in my family, if you're over twenty and not married, you're a spinster!"

"What does your agent think about the wedding?"

"Believe me, he's way more freaked out about this than I am."

"He's afraid the marriage won't last?"

Caprice broke into a laugh. "You've got it backwards, hun. Marriage is good for business. So are kids. Haven't you heard?" she said sarcastically. "Celebrity pregnancies are all the rage!"

"What does ER have to say about everything? I mean, is he happy about this?"

"He just doesn't want to lose me. If I told him I wanted to live on a desert island and raise iguanas for the rest of my life, he'd go along with it," she said, twirling her engagement ring. Very few things in my life have taken my breath away, but when Caprice first showed me her engagement ring, I was stunned into silence. The only other place I'd ever seen a 9.999-carat radiant diamond solitaire on a band of white pavé diamonds was at the Smithsonian.

"You don't have to do this, you know," I pushed, trying to sound as convincing as possible, knowing I was no match for the military-bridal complex seated in the next room.

Caprice rolled her eyes.

"It's too late. His mother has already hired the wedding planner and booked the hotels and caterer, and then there's the dress. She even went with me to Paris for it. All *I* have to do is show up."

I was about to launch into my "break with traditions" speech—the one Evie is so good at—when my cell phone rang.

The caller ID simply read: SHE. I clicked talk and without skipping a beat, the voice on the other end simply said, "This is Jools from Sheila Hicks's office. How soon can you get here?"

Jools!" The petite powerhouse of a woman barked into her Bluetooth headset. "Get me Clooney, Scorsese, and Spielberg—in that order." Gnomish in stature, with beauty-parlor-styled hair and more than a few curves to go around, Sheila Hicks was clearly a force to be reckoned with.

While her assistant, Jools, placed the calls from an outer office, her second assistant hurriedly placed a neat stack of mail on a chrome-edged corner of Sheila's Italian burl desk,

moving aside a framed memo entitled "The Rules."

I had Googled Sheila at the spa before running out on Caprice—who totally understood my hasty departure and promised to explain everything to Evie and make sure she had a ride back to the hotel after the shower ended. After all, destiny waits for no man (or man*iac*).

By all accounts, Sheila Hicks was a Hollywood institution. Having worked her way up the ladder of success through sheer strength of will, she'd become the first female agent to break through Hollywood's glass ceiling. And with a roster of clients that made up half of the world's box-office star power, she was considered, by Hollywood insiders, more famous than her famous clients.

To say I was shocked when Jools called was an understatement. I'd never expected Chrissy's friend's friend's hairdresser to come through. The possibility of getting discovered hadn't even entered my brain when Evie and I had planned this trip to La-La Land. Yet here I was, nestled into some powerhouse agent's overstuffed sofa, sipping bottled water, and staring at walls covered with movie posters from just about every blockbuster made in the past ten years. Across the room from me, Sheila prattled into her headset about numbers, grosses, bottom lines, and net profit participations, using dialogue straight out of an old B movie. Judging from the pile of scripts on her desk, she was no doubt brokering blockbusters for the next ten years as well.

Finally she dropped her headset on her desk and shuffled over to greet me, arms open wide for a hug, like she'd known me a million years or something.

"I'm sorry to have kept you waiting, but business comes first. Am I right?" she said, speaking more as an emanation than a flesh-and-blood human being,

I nodded my agreement, feeling completely at a loss for words, due to a sudden onset of the *I'm out of my depth heebie-jeebies*.

"Listen, I've spent all afternoon thinking about your project, dear, and I have only one word for it: brilliant!" Her broad Cheshire cat smile seemed genuine, though like the Cheshire cat, I had the feeling it could fade at a moment's notice.

"Repressive parents. Quirky BFF. What could be more *now*? Am I right?"

"Right." I took a sip of water, rubbed my dry lips together, and again nodded in agreement, although I wasn't so sure that time.

"Your blog—so precious. I especially liked reading about when you inadvertently included those photos from the science fiction convention into your forecast book, mistakenly resulting in the 'Future Shock' trend! Ah . . . people are such followers." She chuckled.

She then moved around her desk, pulled a plastic cigarette

holder (sans cigarette) from the back of her frosted, cotton-candy-coiffed hair, and sat on the edge of the desk to face me.

"For one so young," she said, "you've certainly had your share of adventure, haven't you?"

"I try to stay active." OMG, could I say anything more meaningless?

Now she was pacing. "Let me explain something to you. In order for your life to be a movie—"

"A movie?" I interrupted midgulp, taking an off-ramp into uncharted emotional territory.

"Yes, a movie. That's what I do. What did you think I was talking about?"

"A movie about me?"

"Do you see anyone else in this room?"

Despite the subarctic air-conditioning, a microscopic droplet of sweat trickled down the nape of my neck. "But I barely have one. A life, I mean."

Sheila stopped pacing and stared at me as if I were Marlon Brando (her first client) in a bunny suit.

"I'm sorry," she said, clearly annoyed. "I thought I was speaking to Hautelaw Girl! The girl with the cool video blog, the Paris adventures, and the 'Daily Oblation' fashion column with thousands of devoted readers."

"It's 'Daily Obsession,' and I only have a couple hundred—"

"And the crazy friends, and the sexy Italian boyfriend! Isn't that who you are?!"

"Well . . ." Suddenly my life sounded *a lot* bigger.

"You're being way too humble, my dear. *Waaaay* too

humble! Allow me to enlighten you," she said, grabbing the aforementioned frame from her desk and holding it in front of my face.

"It's right here. Hollywood Rule Number Ten: Nobody *ever* makes it in this business by being humble."

I stared at the framed page. Aside from the title, it was empty.

"But there's nothing there," I said.

"Of course," she replied, placing the frame back down and casually refitting her headset to her ear. "That's because I make the rules in this town! Now, about your project, there will be some minor changes to the story. It needs to be plausible, you know. Like it really happened."

"But it *did* really happen."

"Of course *I* know it did, and *you* know it did. Now we have to convince the rest of the world."

I had no idea what she meant by that, but I dared not ask.

"Now, the first thing to do is assign a writer."

"What for?"

"Think *ink*, dear. Unless you have a better idea, someone will have to write the screenplay. Capeesh?"

"Well, I do keep a journal."

Her eyes lit up. Or should I say darkened, much like a shark's at the first scent of blood.

"Perhaps I've overlooked something." Her Cheshire cat grin returned. "This may turn out better than I thought. This could be big. Big! Hollywood Rule Number Sixteen: Make your own opportunities."

It was all I could do to keep from squealing my head off,

because "It's better to receive" receptors were beginning to crackle through my brain. Was this really happening to me? Me, the poor little rich girl from Greenwich? Was it true that the most powerful superagent in Hollywood was actually interested in making my journal, my video blog, my diary . . . *me*, a movie?!

"We'll need an outline, and maybe some dialogue to look at within the next few days, dear." She tilted her glasses to take a better look at me. "How long did you say you'd be in L.A.?"

"Two weeks."

"Hmmmm, that's not much time."

Jools poked her head in.

"Sheila, Master Ji, your hapkido instructor, is here. And Will is calling again about the folder he dropped off last week."

"Tell that pest if he doesn't drop dead in the next five minutes, I'm canceling his contract!" Sheila said, clearly rankled. "Tell him to come get it. The next time I want to look at someone's scrapbook, I'll call my five-year-old nephew. Even he knows more about pitching a movie than that idiot!"

Jools nodded dutifully, then closed the door again, leaving us once more.

Sheila took a deep breath and said, "I'm having a little get-together at my place tonight. Sort of a birthday celebration for my favorite person on earth."

"Your husband?"

"Oh, God no! He ran off with his tennis coach years ago. No, I'm talking about *me*, dear."

"Well, happy birthday!"

"Save it for this evening. It will be just a few industry people, Madonna, Cruise, maybe De Niro, cake, and shoptalk, that sort of thing. You should be there. There are people I'll want to meet you. My parties are the essence of my technique — much easier doing business in a social setting than an office."

Wow. Evie was going to freak!

"Can I bring my friend?"

"The quirky BFF? Absolutely! Jools will give you my info."

"What should I wear?"

She paused a moment to consider the question, then smiled with a flash of teeth and said, "Now would be a good time to tell you Hollywood Rule Number Two: Perception is everything!"

left, smiling out loud, which I'm known to do for no apparent reason from time to time. But this time my smile was because what had just happened made me feel like I was walking into Barneys with a fifty-thousand-dollar gift certificate.

I flashed back to my original vision of my future. All this time my ambition had been to become the huge fashion goddess that I know is lurking down in my soul. But could I have been wrong all these years? Was my true destiny something bigger, sparklier, more silver screened? Maybe my vision needed a makeover — a future refashioning of sorts. In fact, maybe Sheila was just what the doctor ordered.

chapter five

We're off to See the Wizard...

date: MARCH 13, 5:00 P.M.
mood: HAPPY!

Mes chéries,
Happy Easter, Happy Passover, and while I'm at it,
Merry Chrismukkah! (Just in case I missed any of you
in December.)
Heart,
Imogene

Comments: 3

—Will someone in Broadband Hollywoodland just give
Hautelaw Girl and her sidekick, Evie, their own show
already? —Posted by Anonymous

—Hello, Hautelaw Girl. I think your life would make a great movie. =]] —Posted by Samantha

—I know for a fact that this is a fake video blog created by wannabe Hollywood types. Really nice going, gals—great props and wardrobe!—Posted by Iris!

✳   ✳   ✳

Evie, resplendent in a trend-transformed little black dress that she'd painstakingly embroidered with beautiful rice paper dolls she'd created herself, lay sprawled across the downy, king-size hotel bed, with one eye on a tabloid magazine and the other on my sixth frantic wardrobe change.

I frowned at my reflection in the mirror (or as Evie referred to it, the flaw-o-meter) and peeled the last of my outfit inventory pictures off the closet door. (Random fact re: *moi*—I keep a scrapbook filled with movable digital pictures containing every piece of clothing, every shoe, and every accessory I own—dated, cross-referenced, and annotated.)

The problem was, I wasn't sure which inner persona to channel. (There were so many, after all.) But after an hour or so of pulling clothes down off hangers, trying on outfit after outfit—none of which were right—I finally went with "gorjus," selecting a pink silk Peter Som halter and a Devi Kroell metallic snakeskin clutch. (Cue the sparkle!) Actually, my outfit was so gorgeous, it came with an invisible disclaimer. *Caution: May cause sudden heart palpitations!* Perfect for Sheila's party, not to mention Hollywood Rule Number Two.

Evie flipped a page of *Us Weekly* and asked absently, "So, what did she say again?"

I'd only gone over this with her a hundred times in the past hour. It wasn't that she forgot, it was that it wasn't sinking in.

"That she thinks someone may want to make a movie about *moi*. I'm supposed to write a couple of scenes for her to show to producers. Nothing big, just a few snippets from my life with some dialogue thrown in so that she can hear my 'voice' and get a feel for Hautelaw Girl."

"Who?" Evie sighed, touching her finger to her tongue and turning another page. Clearly my life story didn't hold a candle to the Olsen twins.

"That would be me," I huffed.

Evie looked up at me blankly as I cantilevered my torso over her splayed body to retrieve the hotel phone, very nearly creating a new yoga pose in the process.

"That is too crazy for even me to comprehend," she said. "Do you realize that nothing this exciting has happened to anyone from Greenwich since Grace Lombard eloped with a

42

fortune-hunting playboy in 1922? Unbeknownst to Grace, her new husband planned to sell the story to get back his job as a newspaper reporter, but instead fell madly in love with her. They went on to write the story together, and it wound up sweeping the Academy Awards!"

Here's the thing about Evie: She could tell you everything you ever wanted to know about any movie you could think of, down to the tiniest detail—even the craft service caterer (no surprises there).

I dialed Paolo, ready to expound a deeply meaningful sentiment.

On the second ring, I began composing a mental message in case I got his voice mail. I took a deep breath. At the fourth ring, I recounted in my head how the recent events have unfurled. For all you detail-oriented Virgo types out there, here's the historical time line:

Four days ago: Lay in bed wide awake,
wondering if I should raise hamsters for a living.

Twenty-two hours ago:
Called the concierge to book eyelash extensions appointment.
(It's said to increase one's balance.)

Twelve hours ago: OMG!
A real Hollywood agent is interested in moi?

Three minutes ago:
Said Hollywood agent called to say she's ready

to set up meetings, and everyone she's spoken with is excited,
excited, excited to meet me!!

One nanosecond ago:
"Pleez-ah leef your me-saj ahf-ta da beep. . . ."

*   *   *

God, I loved hearing his voice. (Goose bumps!)

"You know, if they make your life into a movie, I can do the costumes! Just like Adrianna Heath!"

"Shhhhhh! You're distracting me!" Sometimes Evie had the worst timing.

Distracted, I blathered something completely unromantic into Paolo's voice mail and hung up, vowing to call him after the party.

Evie sat up. She finally looked excited. "Really, girlena, this is too perfect! Your script and my costumes, think of it," she said. "This could be the biggest thing that's ever happened to us. And of course it will be a complete hit. I mean, who wouldn't want to see a movie about us?"

"And Paolo!"

"We'll be famous!"

Webster's dictionary defines the word "fanatic" as a person with "excessive enthusiasm for and intense devotion to a cause or idea." I mention this because, in spite of being late for the party, Evie *insisted* on taking a detour through Bel Air to ogle some movie stars'

homes—specifically the former domicile of the gone-but-not-forgotten screen diva Zsa Zsa Von Teese.

As an isolated incident this would not have been a problem, but since day one in L.A., she hasn't gone anywhere without her star maps. Don't get me wrong, I like to encourage people with hobbies, like canasta, or bee-keeping, or shoe shopping, but that's not what I'm talking about. I'm talking about the kind of hobby that leads to, shall we say, an unreasonable zeal for its subject matter. I'm talking about hobbies gone *B-A-D*.

It was nearly dusk when we finally parked in front of a massive, ivy-covered gate at the top of Stone Canyon Road. Beyond it, an expanse of tastefully shabby grass blanketed a rolling hill just slightly smaller than Ecuador. At the crest, a lush, bougainvillea-draped, Mediterranean-style villa rested comfortably in perpetual shade, surrounded by ancient white alder trees and clusters of bamboo.

"Can you believe it, girlena? Zsa Zsa used to live right here!"

Evie leaped out of the car and rushed to the front gate, with my camcorder at the ready. Toy looked up at me and sneezed.

"Okay, Toy boy, you wait here," I said. "I have to go make sure your aunt Evie doesn't hurt herself."

I found Evie standing on tiptoes, frantically trying to peer through the centuries of layered ivy.

"The house was built for her in 1929 by her first husband," she heaved, trying to yank a vine worthy of Tarzan out of the way. "He disappeared a few years later while boating in Kenya with his producer. The press suspected foul play, but nothing was ever proved."

"Don't people usually go on safaris in places like that?"

"That's what was so suspicious," she replied, pushing the camera at me. "Shoot me in front of the gate, okay?"

"Only if you do Veronica Lake." I laughed.

Even in the fourth grade, Evie did a fabulous Veronica Lake, peekaboo hair and all.

She tossed her hair forward, turned her head slightly skyward with a meaningful yet vacant look, and leaned against the ivy gate.

"I'm ready for my close-up, Mr. DeMille," she purred . . . then disappeared. I stared through the lens in disbelief— the gate was there, the vines were there, but Evie was gone.

"Evie?" I rushed forward, staring at the wall of ivy in a blind panic.

Suddenly a head popped out next to me. "Check it out. There's an opening in the gate!"

"Ohmigod, Evie! You almost gave me a heart attack!" I gasped.

"You know what this means, of course."

"FOR-GET IT! I am *not* going in there!"

"I read somewhere that Zsa Zsa was a real dog lover and had a swimming pool built in the shape of a dog bone."

"No!" I reiterated. But I could already feel my iron will beginning to bend.

"Furthermore, I don't think there's anyone home."

"How can you tell?"

"Well, if you were on this side of the fence, you could see for yourself."

I reluctantly followed Evie through the opening. Okay, so my iron will is made of Play-Doh. In fact, I have no iron will at all. It's a complete myth.

"*See.* The house is *totally* dark," Evie whispered.

"Because the house is totally in the shade, Evie. Besides, if no one's home, why are you whispering?"

"*Puleeease*, girlena! This is a once-in-a-lifetime opportunity. Give me the camera. I'll just get a quick shot of the pool and we'll go. Promise."

We snuck across the yard using a row of bamboo trees as cover. For my part, I was hovering somewhere between the fear of being caught by the police and the horror of being devoured by some Hound of the Baskervilles–type mongrel left to starve when Zsa Zsa sold the house some seventy years earlier.

Anyway, the trip was worth it, because when we finally crept into the backyard, we were greeted by an Olympic-size dog bone. Pools à la L.A. were clearly symbolic of one's own personal predilections.

Evie started filming, "What did I tell you?" she said proudly.

"Wow!" I cried, completely forgetting about the Hound of the Baskervilles. "This would suit Toy to a T!"

"Who's Toy?" said a voice behind us.

We whirled around and saw a guy standing in the patio doorway. He was a scruffy blond, about six-two, and was clad in a T-shirt, well-worn Levis, and snakeskin cowboy boots. If I had to, I'd compare him to Brad Pitt in *Thelma and Louise*. Very cute!

Evie and I just stared, unable to speak.

"I'm sorry," he continued, "did you ring the front doorbell? Sometimes I can't hear it in the back of the house."

"The front door?" I repeated, stalling for time.

"It's in the front of the house," he said.

"Right."

"Look," he said, "I'm kinda in a hurry. Why don't you come inside and I'll introduce you."

Evie stared at me. I stared at Evie. He stared at both of us.

"We prefer the great outdoors," I blurted.

"Suit yourself." He shrugged, then shouted into the house. "Hannah! Holly! Lee!"

There was a brief ruckus inside, followed by a pile of Pekingese, who all at once barreled onto the patio.

"Meet Hannah and her sisters." He grinned. "And I'm Jace."

"I'm Imogene. And this is Evie."

"I'm surprised the service sent two of you. I mean, they're always griping about being shorthanded. And you're so well dressed. You look like you're going to a party."

"We just left one." I chuckled nervously.

"What service?" Evie asked.

I had a sudden urge to kick her.

"Aren't you from Pooch People?" Jace asked.

"Pooch People. Yes! We're definitely *Pooch People*!" I said, nodding. (Well, we are!)

I glared at Evie. "Don't mind her, she's a trainee."

"A trainee? Wow, that's great! And you guys left a party for this?"

"Yep," I said. "We got the call and, well . . . here we are."

"I'm really impressed with your dedication. Between you and me, the quality of pet sitters has really gone downhill lately. Present company excluded, of course."

Evie shook her head in sympathy. "We know what you mean. We could tell you stories."

Jace glanced at his watch and winced. "I'd love to hear them, but I'm late for a meeting. Listen, there are all kinds of herbal teas in the fridge and plenty to eat—organic, of course.

"The dogs have already been fed. *Just keep them out of the pool*, okay?"

"No problem," Evie and I said in unison.

"Well then, I guess that's it. I'll see you Pooch People later."

Before we had a chance to protest, he vanished around the side of the house, leaving the two of us to ponder the strange and mystical happenstances in the life of a trespasser.

"Not to put too fine a point on this, Evie, but what do we do now?" I seethed. "And what are we going to do with these dogs?"

"Don't worry, girlena. I have a cunning plan."

A pair of tuxedoed sentries waved us through Sheila's double wrought-iron gates and up a long, steep, pebbled driveway lined with majestic old cedars. Sheila's house was the last house on the lane. There was nothing beyond it, unless you count the Pacific Ocean.

Inside was another ocean—*of motion*. Everywhere, chic, sexy people churned and writhed in heated syncopation to a house mix of hip-hop.

I half squeezed, half danced my way through the crush, checking out the locals for what was hot and what was hotter. It was impossible not to overhear a few choice snippets of conversation as we crossed the room. You know, stuff like how good (or not) someone's butt looks in their vintage Fioruccis, new diets, old diets, the latest pharmacosmetic products, not to mention tidbits like:

"Nice to see you."

"Nice to be seen."

And:

"I couldn't walk through the front door until I figured out what my motivation was."

The few who weren't dancing sat chatting on cushy banks of Italian modern sofas pressed against the vast, floor-to-ceiling windows that overlooked the ocean.

Of course Evie, little scandal antenna that she was, honed in on a semiprivate tête-à-tête between a former hip-hop artist turned sitcom star and a former sitcom star turned pop artist about a former dramedy star whose BFF was selling off her deepest and darkest to one of the tabloids. She ditched me when they headed for the bar, leaving me stranded and swaying to the music (like a dork) all by myself—a completely unacceptable situation. I decided this would be as good a time as any to search for Sheila, so I spent the next twenty minutes going from room to room, doing exactly that.

Sheila's home was almost an exact replica of my beloved Malibu Barbie Dream House. The basic design— midcentury modern, complete with walls of glass and a cantilevered rock roof—jutted way out over the peninsula's precipice. Have I mentioned my acrophobia yet? I mean, it was like the architect had totally missed the e-mail about the Pacific Rim. You know, earthquakes, Richter scales, homes on the edge of cliffs falling into the ocean—that one!

Unfortunately, I felt completely out of place. My first Hollywood party had me anything but calm, cool, and collected. I could feel my insecurities take over: *I am totally out of my depth here with all these movie biggies.* Before going any farther, I decided to just take a few minutes to compose myself.

Luckily, I spotted a terrace. It was warm outside, almost

balmy this close to the ocean, and amazingly clear. A sliver of crescent moon, crisp and luminous, hovered over a host of laurel trees that punctuated the landscape. The scent of night-blooming jasmine hung in the air. Everything about the moment was intoxicating, and I understood then why so many people who come here to visit never leave.

The soft evening breeze aroused an unidentified yearning inside me. All at once I had an overriding urge to call Paolo. . . . How I missed him! But that thought came to an end abruptly when a chorus of coyote howls echoed from a distant canyon.

I hugged myself, wondering how close they actually were.

"Don't worry," a deep voice behind me said. "They're actually far away."

I spun around as a figure stepped out of the shadows and into the moonlight. I was stunned and disoriented when he came into full view—he was the second most beautiful man I'd ever seen. Had he been there the whole time?

"They're smart," the mystery man continued. "They stay away from us humans. They know how dangerous we can be."

"I . . . I didn't know I wasn't alone out here," I stuttered, a bit unhinged by his good looks. Not only that, he looked familiar. I tried placing him. I knew his face, but how? From where?

"My apologies," he said with a rueful smile. "You seemed so peaceful standing there. I didn't mean to disturb you."

I didn't know what to say. And I probably stared for longer than I should have. I couldn't help it. His skin gleamed with all the radiance of a thousand Swarovski crystals, while his dazzling smile vied for glory with his other heavenly features.

There was a long pause as he waited for me to say something. But I couldn't. I was completely mesmerized.

Slowly he took a sip of champagne, carefully studying me through eyes more brilliant than fire opals. I flashed on random factoids about that particular gemstone—a topic every fashionista worth her salt knows a thing or two about: *Fire opals were unparalleled in ancient times and were symbols of the most impassioned love. The Indians of Central America believed that anything that sparkled with such intense vivacity as the fire opal could only have been created in the waters of paradise. . . .*

"You seem to be at a loss for words," he said.

A wave of his mahogany hair caught a glint of moonlight as he moved closer to me. "Or is this some type of new get-acquainted tactic I haven't heard of yet? Get the other person to reveal as much as they possibly can about themselves before deciding whether you want to talk to them or not. Slick. Okay, I'll bite. I'm Dustin." He smiled, extending his hand. "I enjoy mountain biking, clubbing, and long walks on the beach. And you?"

"Um . . ." Did I mention what a great wit I am? I mean, this happens every time I get near a guy this perfect. Call it what you like: biorhythms, synchronicity, or magnetic attraction. It doesn't really matter, because the end result is always the same: a complete loss of nerve followed by vocal incapacitation. In other words, I freeze up. The same thing happened when I met Paolo. Oops. Best not to go there now.

We stared at each other a few more seconds. I must have swallowed wrong, because suddenly I began having trouble breathing. Dustin, picking up on my overwhelming spaz attack, took a step toward me and placed a firm hand gently on my back.

"Inhale," he instructed, looking seriously concerned.

I followed his instructions precisely, praying my breathing wouldn't morph into hyperventilation.

When I recovered, he smiled at me patiently, giving me another chance.

"I have an idea." From the inside pocket of his expensive leather jacket, he removed a Mont Blanc pen. He scribbled some numbers on a cocktail napkin and handed it to me.

"Maybe you'd be more relaxed talking to me on the phone. I'll go over there," he said, pointing to the corner of the terrace, "and you call me. We'll have a nice get-to-know-each-other chat."

I shook my head and surprised myself when a giggle escaped. "Thanks, I'll be okay. I'm just a little overwhelmed by the party and everything. And I was trying to figure out why you look so familiar."

"I'll take that as a compliment. You probably remember me from *The Vampire Diaries*. I played the rogue priest killed by a stray silver bullet in the middle of act two." He clutched his heart and winced.

"I thought those only worked on werewolves."

"That's what they want you to believe." He inched closer. "Or maybe you remember me as agent Dirk Masters in *Enemy*

Blue, a Cold War thriller on a modest budget —*very* modest.

"Let me guess," I said. "You take a bullet for your country."

"Cyanide, I'm afraid." He raised his glass and took a last sip.

I laughed. He was very close now.

He lowered his eyelids and spoke ever so softly. "But in real life, I'm just a regular guy with a soft spot for puppies and beautiful women."

His expression went still. He lifted my chin with a finger and fluttered the lightest kiss across my cheek. Though I'm not one hundred percent sure, I could swear I detected my knee wobble.

I had an unexpected urge to invite him back to my hotel room to watch *Love Story*. Instead I stiffened. Dual emotions fought for my attention: On one hand, I was completely mesmerized by Dustin. On the other, I felt ashamed of that. Not two minutes ago I had been pining for Paolo. Now, suddenly, I felt almost glad that he wasn't here.

"Are you all right?" Dustin asked softly. Gently.

"Sorry," I replied, brushing away his concern. "I'm just, um . . . preoccupied."

I shivered and with that he removed his jacket and slipped it carefully over my shoulders, revealing a lean yet powerful musculature, which with even the slightest of movements rippled beneath the perfect fit of his whisper-thin cashmere sweater.

After I slipped my arms into the jacket sleeves, he took a step back to study me. He knit his eyebrows together in consternation, though behind it I detected a faint smile. I could tell he was working hard to suppress a laugh. I looked down at myself—at what he saw. The sleeves alone came practically to my hips, making me look totally elfin. It's not that I was small, it's that *he was so tall.*

Finally he gave in to his laugh. I laughed too. But our mirth was short-lived, when a new mood appeared in his face. He stepped closer—so close I could feel his lighter-than-air breath. And then something strange happened. I felt myself getting dizzy. Everything around me began to swirl. All I could focus on were his soft, sweet lips just inches from mine. But just as I felt myself slipping away to paradise, the terrace door slid open.

"HEY!" Evie shouted. I pulled away and faced her. Evie's arrival obscured the delicate moment, which was now gone. The eclipse enabled me to process what had just happened. Then the guilt hit. *I mean, we were just talking innocently . . . then he began flirting. And lo and behold, I flirted back. . . . OMG, why did I do that? I could have tried giving him the death look, but he just kept smiling. I can't believe I almost kissed him!*

"I've been looking all over for you." Evie's eyes grew wide.

"This is my friend Evie," I said, nervously twirling my heart-shaped aquamarine earrings—*the ones Paolo gave me!*

"*Enchanté,*" Dustin said, smiling, reaching for Evie's hand.

And then it dawned on me—I hadn't introduced myself. "And I'm Imogene."

"I know."

Before *that* could register, I noticed Evie and how she had

56

been surveying Dustin. A discreet glance for Evie was totally out of the question. No—Evie gawked.

"Aren't you Dustin Litchfield? The actor?!" Evie gushed. I knew any minute she'd be all over him with a thousand embarrassing personal questions, pleas for insider gossip, autograph requests, and a host of other crazy Evie *things*. I had to intervene.

"Well, it was nice meeting you," I said, briskly turning on my heels. "Good-bye."

His expressive eyes clouded over.

"Good-bye sounds so final. How about 'I'll call you tomorrow'? You did keep my number, I hope."

"Oh. Yes," I said, blushing. "Of course."

Evie stared at me as if to say, *Girlena, you devil.* I grasped Evie's hand, and we began to walk away. And in an effort to prevent her from looking back, I gave her arm an extra tug. Though I couldn't help a last look back over my own shoulder. As we faded into the crowd, Dustin's hand lingered in the air, and I secretly hoped that it *wasn't* a last good-bye.

Evie and I wandered over to the mile-long buffet table by the pool and perused the magnificent tiara-topped birthday cake. Yum! Suffice it to say, my diet regime had flown out the window—after all, how bad can a bit of buttercream be for the body, when it's so good for the soul?

Evie disappeared again, following after an outfit she just had to admire at close range, so I grabbed a slice of

cake and resumed my search for Sheila, keeping both eyes fixed on the incredibly buff swimmers (just in case she was hiding among them). Sadly, this left no eyes for the guy standing directly in front of me, whose back I plowed into, cake and all, sending him sprawling onto a nearby table. It shot into the pool with him on top, dragging two guests, a waiter, and a chow chow with it.

After a hearty round of applause, a phalanx of waiters magically appeared and began pulling the guests out of the deep end. I grabbed a towel and rushed over to make my apologies.

"OHMIGOD! I'm so . . ." I stopped mid-apology as the guy climbed onto the deck and stood up to face me. It was Jace. The dog manny!

He snatched the towel and wiped off his face. It was an unhappy face. Especially after he recognized me.

"Wait a minute, you're that Pooch Person," he said, turning red with anger. "What are you doing here? And what have you done with the dogs?"

"The dogs?"

As it turned out, Evie's cunning plan was nothing short of dognapping. It entailed bringing the Pekingese to the party, leaving them in the car with Toy (a remarkably responsible animal) in charge, and sneaking them back in through the gate on the way home—all without encountering their owners or Jace in the process. No doubt there's a law against doing things like this; with my luck, it'll be a federal crime, and I'll go to jail for life. How do I always let myself get talked into these things?

"Yeah, the dogs," Jace growled. "You're supposed to be watching them — *remember?*"

"They're in good hands," I assured him.

"Don't tell me you left them with that trainee!"

"Trainee? Oh, right, Evie! Yes, she's watching them."

Jace shook his soaking head. "I've gotta find a new job. This is way too stressful. What are *you* doing here, anyway?"

"What's that supposed to mean?"

"Hey, no offense, but you don't exactly strike me as L.A. party circuit material."

"*Really?* Well, as it so happens, I was invited by Sheila herself."

"Sure you were," he scoffed.

"What about you? Aren't you supposed to be at a meeting?"

"Not that I need to justify my whereabouts to you, but if you must know, I'm *meeting* someone *here*, to talk about a part. Well, I *was*, anyway. Thanks to you, unless it's the part of Flipper, I'm screwed!"

"Yeah, right. You're probably just here for the free food."

"Listen," he said, sizing me up, "whatever your name is — "

"It's Imogene."

"Fine. If I were you I'd make damn sure nothing happens to those dogs."

"That's some pretty tough talk for a *dog nanny!*"

"It's dog *manny!*"

"Whatever. What are you going to do, call the pooch police?"

"As it happens, the owner of that house is Milos Meltzer, the hottest director on the planet right now. He also happens to be returning from a location scout in Rome sometime around eleven. Oh, and he's crazy about those dogs."

"Relax, they're fine."

As if on cue, Hannah and her sisters chose that precise moment to come barreling through the crowd.

Guests squealed as the rogue dog pack cut a wide swath through the mob, making a beeline for the pool. I raced toward them, planting myself directly in their path.

One question. How did they get out of the car?

"Stop!" I hollered, flailing my arms like a maniac.

Jace shouted, "No! Not the pool!"

But it was too late. Hannah and her devoted siblings plunged into the water like Olympic swimmers, followed by Jace, for the second time that evening. Toy, on the other hand, jumped straight into my arms.

Everyone howled uncontrollably as Jace fished the dogs out one by one. Their once gorgeous blond hair had suddenly turned a hideous shade of neon green. Who knew dogs had highlights? And if there's one thing every-one who has highlights knows, chlorine is your enemy.

Jace was beside himself at best. Ignoring my apology, he did what any responsible dog manny would do under the circumstances. He stormed off.

Votive candles encircled the area where I found Evie chilling, oblivious to the Pekingese pool-party panic she'd just missed. Cushy, outdoor double-width chaise lounges served as seating, and an oversize, larger-than-life, retractable projection screen dominated the view.

"Hey, girlena! Check out this outdoor screening room!" Evie hollered. "And this," she added, gesturing to the vast selection of movie candy that filled the authentic showcase. And as if that wasn't enough, there was a freestanding popcorn maker, a soda fountain, and a cotton candy machine.

Evie grinned. I was livid. After relaying the escape of Hannah and her sisters, I asked the obvious question: "How did those dogs get out of the car?"

"Dogs need air!"

"I know, Evie, but you only had to leave the window open a crack."

"One man's crack is another man's —"

"Whatever!" I said, exasperated. Evie's outré logic prevailed, and I knew there was no point arguing with her, or prolonging my pain any longer. I just wanted to find Sheila, say hi, and go home.

"Evie, we have to go."

"Go? I just got here," she said, planting herself on a low teak table under one of a dozen ornamental paper lanterns.

"Yeah, what's the rush?" A girl's head popped up from

one of the chaise lounges, followed by a second one right next to hers.

"Oh, Imogene, this is Ashlie and Mia," Evie said, juggling a handful of Raisinets and a handful of Milk Duds.

Giggles ensued from the chaise longues.

"Can you believe it? Mia's dad is Milos Meltzer—you know, the producer!"

Oh, great. The dogs' owner.

Mia frowned. "Didn't I see you chatting with Jace?"

"Aka, just another Hollywood extra with delusions of grandeur," Ashlie added.

"Are you a friend of his? Because he's Daddy's dog manny."

"Not anymore," I mumbled. I decided to change the subject. "Is your father really Milos Meltzer? *Remember Us* is one of my all-time favorite films!" I gushed.

Ashlie tilted her head and studied me, "You know, you look just like that girl on the Internet."

"Oh, Ash, you're totally right," said Mia, twirling a knuckleful of jewel-encrusted stackable rings. "What *is* her name?"

"Hautelaw Girl," Evie announced. "That's really Imogene."

I decided to wait until Evie finished her Milk Duds before I killed her.

"Shut up." Mia perked up. "I read your blog, like, all the time."

"Me too," added Ashlie. "It's awesome! Especially your trip to Paris. Like, completely brilliant."

How weird. No one at home makes a big deal over it, so why these alpha daughters would was beyond me. But I guess I liked it just the same. Okay, maybe I'd let Evie live. Admittedly, I could get used to the kind of notoriety you get out here. Back East you practically had to win a Nobel Prize before anyone paid the slightest bit of attention to you. But out here all you had to do was blog.

"So what brings you to L.A.?" Mia asked.

"Evie and I are doing Fashion Fantasy Camp."

"Really? How fun! Is that how you know Sheila?"

"No. I met her through a mutual friend."

"You're totally lucky, because nobody *ever* gets invited to her parties."

It seemed rude to ask where all the people at the party *had* come from.

"Unless she's, like, doing business with you," Ashlie said with renewed interest.

"Are you?" asked Mia.

"Maybe. I don't know."

"She means yes," said Evie.

"How fun!" said Ashlie. "If you're going to be working with Sheila, we can hang out."

"Yeah, we were just trying to decide on a movie to put in. A vintage one," Mia said.

"What about *Annie Hall*?" Evie suggested.

"Ew. I *never* watch black-and-white movies," said Ashlie. "I don't understand them."

"Forget the movie," Mia said. "Let's go out! There's a new club on the strip, Hypno. A friend of ours owns it. Why don't you come along?"

"Absolutely!" Evie said.

"We'd love to, but we can't," I said.

"We can't?" Evie echoed. "Why not?"

I really had to go find Sheila.

"Actually, I shouldn't be going anywhere. I have an early morning with my personal trainer. She'll absolutely lose it if I blow her off again. Besides, I can't bear these thunder thighs a moment longer," Mia said, pinching a microscopic portion of skin.

"Oh God," Evie teased. "Fake body issues are so last season." She gave Mia a playful nudge.

I started to laugh when I noticed a hint of annoyance curl around Mia's downturned lips. The sudden silence felt awkward.

Evie's expression revealed her regret and confusion. Clearly, her brain was deciphering just how deeply she'd messed up, and what the ramifications were, having fallen out of favor with what I took to be one of L.A.'s A-list party girls. Now I got why the pools here were filled with Kabbalah water—I mean, how completely necessary daily purification on a large scale would be in a place like this.

Given all that, I wondered what the best strategy would be. Would Evie start babbling to cover her mistake, or change the subject in hopes of moving past it? No one said another word. This would really, really be a good time to take off.

I reached for Evie. "You wouldn't happen to know where I could find Sheila, would you?" I asked Mia and Ashlie.

"She usually holds court in, like, the Pacific wing," Mia said, breaking into a smile as if nothing had happened. "You know, the one that sticks out over the edge of the cliff."

After a brief exchange of e-mail addresses and phone numbers (Mia asked for mine, not Evie's), I rushed Evie into the house, hoping to find our wraps and get us out of there before any more damage could be done.

All I wanted to do was go home, but it was Evie who insisted that I at least show myself to Sheila. According to Evie, our future depended on it. She said she'd catch up with me shortly, so I passed her Toy and went off in search of our hostess once more.

I climbed a spiral staircase in the Pacific wing and found myself in a crowded lounge. I surveyed the room's topography. Mirrors and lights tucked neatly behind modern modular sofas made everything look as if it were floating. A flock of decorative Claude Lalanne faux sheep were strewn here and there amid the Lucite tables filled with champagne flutes, crumpled cocktail napkins, and half-eaten hors d'oeuvres. And there, standing dead center like the queen bee in a hive, was Sheila, chattering away simultaneously with several cliques of power-player types, all of whom buzzed madly around her, hoping to be spoken with next.

I managed to catch her eye (no small miracle), and she waved me over.

"Happy birthday!" I said cheerily.

"Imogene! I'm so glad you could make it!"

I smiled at her warm greeting. It made me feel special among special people. Everyone within earshot or eyeshot turned to look at who might be worthy of such attention.

"Me too."

"Listen, I spoke with Emily and Rebecca Tweed this

afternoon. They have a producing deal at Paramount and they want to meet with you about your project. Tomorrow!" She smiled, pleased with herself to no end. "Jools will arrange everything. Am I fast or what?"

What could I say? I was thoroughly overwhelmed.

"Wow!"

"In the meantime, I've been giving casting a lot of thought, and I've found someone *absolutely perfect* for one of the parts!" Sheila turned her attention to a nearby clique and grabbed someone's elbow, pulling it *and* the body it was attached to toward us. "Imogene, meet your new Paolo!"

For the second time that evening, I found myself staring into the eyes of Dustin Litchfield.

chapter six

Moi, Inc.

Date: March 15
To: My dear devoted "Daily Obsession" readers
From: I, Imogene
Re: Greetings from La-La Land!
I swear on my Chanel Bible that I will e-mail trend alerts
as regularly as possible, as all you die-hard fashion
addicts are lying awake at night awaiting my "Daily
Obsession" missives, even though the next two weeks
begin a new, unbelievable career path for *moi*. To be
continued . . .

E ver since Jack Warner, Louis B. Mayer, and Samuel
Goldwyn crossed the Mojave Desert in search of
the Promised Land, power breakfasts have been the
thing in L.A. And the most powerful power breakfasts of all,
since time immemorial, have happened at the Polo Lounge in

the Beverly Hills Hotel, where Sheila had arranged for me to meet the sister producing team *Twin Tweed*.

As producers go, Emily and Rebecca Tweed were super hot, riding a tsunami of hit films, not to mention a successful new television series.

The moment I sat down at their table, all activity in the restaurant ceased. Everyone glanced, discreetly of course, to see if I was *somebody*, immediately returning to their own breakfasts when I proved to be just another mere mortal.

I scanned the menu, trying to look as if I belonged there. By all accounts I didn't. The room was jammed — mostly with industry types, as best I could tell. Everywhere BlackBerrys tinkled; people seemed to be either pitching or receiving story ideas. Or both. That might sound glamorous, but it all struck me as a tad superficial. I never thought I'd hear myself say this, but by comparison, Greenwich was utterly *deep*.

A waiter appeared.

"Two orders of scrambled egg whites in olive oil, no bread, no potatoes, no dairy. Turkey bacon, double pressed dry," he said as he set down the plates in front of Rebecca and Emily.

"If there's a scintilla of fat on this, I'm sending it back," Rebecca threatened.

"I can assure you, there is not a drop of moisture left — fat or otherwise." He rolled his eyes.

The waiter turned to me. "And eggs Benedict with extra hollandaise," he oozed with relish, deliberately swinging the dish under Rebecca's nose before setting it down before me.

The two sisters fixed their eyes on my plate unhappily as the waiter slipped away.

After the initial small-talk phase, Rebecca Tweed got down to business.

"First of all, we think your concept is great! Country bumpkin makes it in the big city against insurmountable odds."

"A classic fish-out-of-water story," Emily agreed. "It's wonderful."

I must admit, I have been known to get a smidge excitable hearing positive proclamations concerning all things me.

"We were thinking about who could play your mother," Emily continued, rattling off a list of aging sex symbols—none of whom bore the slightest resemblance to my real mother.

I sat in silence, twisting my Love bracelet, stirring my orange juice with the straw, and playing with the bread basket.

"It's got everything . . . comedy, drama, sex, romance. But my sister thinks the protagonist isn't believable enough."

"Huh. But it is a true story," I said softly. I guess the rest of the world viewed my life as a tad unbelievable. Clearly Sheila had been right.

I began thinking about Dustin Litchfield as Paolo. They didn't look anything alike, but there was something similar about them. They were both *very* charming . . . *and* sexy . . . *and* had amazing bodies. But it wasn't just their mutual good looks that made Dustin seem right for the part. What was so similar about them was their intensity. I'd never found that in anyone before Paolo. And haven't seen it in anyone since Dustin. And for me, that passion could prove to be very, very dangerous.

"Look," Emily said, snapping me back into the conversation, "you just don't feel *real* enough."

Oh no, here we go again.

"What's more real than reality?" I asked.

Emily took a bite of egg white and grimaced. "What my sister is trying to say is, well, we were wondering how you'd feel about making the protagonist a superhero?"

"A superhero?"

"Yeah, a *fashion* superhero!"

I couldn't decide whether to laugh at how ridiculous that sounded, or cry because my life wasn't nearly as interesting as people thought it should be.

I took a sip of orange juice and tried to appear open-minded. Maybe it wasn't such a bad idea after all. I mean, I can't even tell you how often I've wished I could move faster than a speeding bullet.

Rebecca carefully forked up the last of her scrambled eggs.

"Sheila tells us you're quite a writer," she said, finally pushing her plate away.

"Well, I . . ."

"I have an idea. Why don't you take a crack at a couple of scenes? Just go with the concept. Let's see what you can come up with."

How can I describe my reaction? In a nutshell: Mouth agape. Awe. Out-of-body experience. Get the picture?

Emily dabbed a napkin to her lips. "We'd *love* to see what you can do with it. I'll call Sheila when we get back to the office. But for now," she said, eyeing her watch, "we have another meeting."

On that note, she abruptly sat back and gave me the old "we're done here, no need to see your face a nano-second longer" smile, while her sister checked an incoming BlackBerry message.

As for me, I politely thanked them, said my good-byes, and headed for the ladies' to slip into my super suit and fly back to Santa Monica. But as I swung the door open, a shoulder plowed into my back.

"Oh, dear, I'm *soooooo* sorry," a voice purred in faux sympathy.

A sickening lump welled up in my throat and I twirled around in dismay. My nemesis, Brooke, smirked behind black-lensed aviators. Their silver rims caught a shard of glittering sunlight through the bathroom window, accentuating her razor-blade cheekbones to a T. *And* speaking of which, if she were wearing one, a T-shirt that is, it would have read HONK IF YOU LOVE SQUASHING THE LITTLE PEOPLE IN YOUR LIFE.

Instead she was dressed in a white Hervé Léger dress, which clung dangerously close to her body. Her legs were tanned the same color as her pointy-studded bag, which looked appropriately like a lethal weapon. If that weren't enough, a Bea Valdes necklace, aptly named "Venom," clung to her throat.

"Hi, Brooke," I said, willing the corners of my mouth to turn upward in the hopes that the jab to my back was an accident. Okay, I admit it, I have a denial thing.

It's one thing running into her in NYC now and again; being that we're three thousand miles from home, this was just too much. But then a cheery thought crossed my mind: Perhaps she's swapping the East Coast for the West! Did I dare hope? Why not? *Yay!*

"What are you doing here?" she said, getting straight to the point.

"I'm doing what everyone else is doing, having breakfast."

"You really are stupid. Nobody comes here to eat. They come here to deal. And judging by the company you're keeping, you're here to deal."

I didn't even have to ask what she was doing here. She'd just answered that question for me.

"What do you mean?" I said as innocently as I possibly could.

Brooke folded her arms and exhaled loudly.

"The Tweed sisters. I've been watching you from across the room."

"I didn't see you."

"That's because I didn't want to be seen — not by you, anyway."

I blinked several times. I just wanted to get away from her. I decided to take the path of least resistance.

"It was just a simple conversation, not that it's any of your business."

"It's bad enough that you're at Fashion Fantasy Camp — not that there's the slightest possibility it will improve your style sense," she said, quickly observing my last-season faux pas. "If I were you," Brooke continued, "I'd pray not to wind up in one of my lectures. On second thought, it might make this ridiculous camp gig entertaining."

I glanced at my watch. Not only did I want to get out of there more than anything else in the world, I had to. I was late for the eleven o'clock lecture, and Evie was holding a seat for me.

"As wonderful as it is to see you again, Brooke, I have to go."

Brooke pushed her face into mine. "I'm warning you, Dorothy, there's only room for one fashion forecaster in this town. You might have gotten lucky when you stole my job at Hautelaw, but don't even think about getting in my way out here."

Consider the crinkle: a bunch of wavy lines that curve and twist like little giggles in physical form. They're fun, whimsical, and lighthearted. They're also something used in fashion to create texture and variety."

This was our eleven a.m. "Inspiration" lecture—where to find it, and how to harness it. Unfortunately for me, I'd missed most of it, thanks to my run-in with Brooke and bumper-to-bumper traffic. Oh well, I knew Evie would fill me in later.

Evie and some other FFC campers were huddled around a table, peering intently at paper plates, each with exactly three crinkle-cut french fries carefully arranged on top.

"Sorry I'm late," I whispered.

Evie snapped her head in the opposite direction. Okay, she was definitely annoyed.

"What's wrong?" I asked.

"Whatever do you mean?" she said, thumping her fingers impatiently over her book, *The 7 Habits of Highly Effective Teens*.

While my brain tried to conjure the perfect excuse to win Evie's forgiveness, our lecturer took a deep breath and summed up.

"My concepts were due any minute. By some miracle I had wandered onto a narrow street and stumbled into a tiny café. There, the kindly owner and his dear wife attended to my every need, bringing me sustenance in the form of a delicious *hamburger de Roquefort* and a basket of freshly cooked french fries. I rallied my strength and reached for a fry, intent on satisfying my savage hunger, but instead of devouring it I stopped and stared in wonder. They weren't the straight-cut fries I had expected, but rather, they were *crinkle cut*. At that moment the bolt of lightning struck! I held the wavy morsel up to the light, tears of joy streaming down my cheeks. I envisioned my entire spring line, crinkled, wrinkled, scalloped, and crimped, gloriously parading before my eyes! I had found my inspiration!"

The room broke into applause as our lecturer took a bow. I gave up trying to communicate with Evie, judging it best to let her anger or annoyance, or whatever it was, run its course. I mean, knowing Evie, that wouldn't take long. She was never the type to hold a grudge, especially with moi.

As we gathered our things to leave, Cory, the head counselor, popped her head in to announce that we had a surprise afternoon special. Everyone would be attending the Tina Lorenz fashion show. The hottest *must-have* ticket in L.A.!

Tina Lorenz was at the heart of L.A.'s newfound couture culture and the darling of the music industry's branding juggernaut, having designed successful clothing lines for many a hip-hop artist.

After circumnavigating the fashion-hungry mob at the door, Evie and I slipped into the back row, a place we P.I.T.s, (formerly Professionally Irrelevant Teens, we've since graduated to Pros in Training), were quite accustomed to.

Thankfully, Evie seemed in better spirits. Her mood swing was clearly the result of an injection of pure fashion energy. I didn't want to ruin anything by bringing up this morning. Besides, it was nice to have her back.

We entertained ourselves by playing Spot the Celeb, as the front rows filled up with actors, rock stars, editors, and brand-name Hollywood stylists.

Evie had just pointed out a child star turned celebrity chef when a woman sporting a two-way phone and clipboard approached us.

"Excuse me, but are you Hautelaw Girl?"

My eyes bugged. (a) Who was she and why did she want to know? and (b) How firsthand embarrassing.

"I guess," I responded hesitantly.

Just then her phone chirped to life. "Have you got her, Sarah?" a voice on the other end crackled.

"I'm with her now," she replied.

"Three minutes," the voice said.

Sarah looked at me and smiled faintly. "Sorry. You must be confused. I'm with Tina Lorenz's company. She'd like you to join some of her friends in the front row."

I was stunned. I mean, *I* didn't know Tina Lorenz. How did she know *me*?

I looked at Evie. Her stony expression was back.

"Um . . . can my friend come too?"

"Sorry. There's only one seat. Madonna was a no-show."

I turned back to Evie. As much as I wanted to stay with her, the chance of sitting up front was too good to miss.

"Evie, will you be okay here without me?"

Evie just stared at me blankly—not a good sign. She wasn't about to understand, no matter how hard I'd try to explain. So I didn't bother. I mean, this was one of those moments where the choice I made might have a profound effect on my entire life. On the one hand, I couldn't possibly abandon Evie. She was my best friend, my soul mate, my single most powerful (parents aside) support group. To leave her now would be a horrible thing to do. And I'd feel guilty about it forever. On the other hand, this was clearly one of those once-in-a-lifetime opportunities. I mean, who knows who I might meet . . . maybe this would be one of those grand, defining life experiences—the kind I'd look back on and say, you know, if I hadn't gone down and sat in that front row, such and such would never have happened. I mean, if the situation were reversed, I'd want *her* to go. No, I'd *make* her go!

"Whatever," Evie snipped, flicking her wrist at me to go.

"Great! I'll meet you after the show," I promised.

Sarah clutched my arm, and I was delivered directly to Richard Hunter—the voice on the other end of the two-way. His look was early Beatles (when they were in their skinny suit phase).

As it turned out, Richard was a rep from Tina's PR firm—or, as he put it, her "praisery"—and was there to help me "meet some people."

"We weren't expecting you to be here or we would have picked you up at your hotel," he said. "Tina's a big fan."

"Of what?" I asked.

Richard laughed (a little too easily, I thought). "Your video blog, Hautelaw Girl. Everybody in L.A. is talking about it."

"Really?"

"*Yuh*," he said, as if everybody in the world already knew that. "It's hot. Very hot."

With that, he escorted me through the crowd, introducing me to a slew of people—people who, before now, I'd only known in their two-dimensional form, by watching their movies and listening to their music. But now they were *real*. I mean, I was actually shaking their hands and talking to them, even being air kissed by them! Next thing I knew, I was sitting next to Oh-Em-Gee, you'll never believe who! *Beyoncé!*

A news crew appeared out of nowhere for a quickie interview: *What is it like to be Hautelaw Girl? How long have Beyoncé and you been friends? What do you think of Tina's work? . . .* That sort of thing.

I could see it all now. Small-town girl (if you call Greenwich a small town), *moi*, Imogene, in hot pursuit of her dreams to become the leading fashion phenomenon in the world, jets to L.A., and within days is thrust into the limelight as she scores a front-row seat with Beyoncé at the hottest fashion show of the century.

No wonder so many people want to be famous. This feeling of being larger than life was beyond hypnotic. My head was still spinning from the camera flashes and reporters crowding around me—everyone calling for me to look their way; everyone wanting me to speak to them. They all wanted my attention. They all wanted me!

When the lights had faded and the show began, I just sat there staring at the models on the runway, and for the first time in my entire life I wasn't paying attention to the clothes or the shoes or the accessories. All I could think about was the rush of excitement from all those people wanting to know Hautelaw Girl. Maybe Hautelaw Girl could be a superhero after all. Maybe she already was.

The Fashion- Forward Adventures of Imogene

* * *

INT. SPRING SOMMER'S OFFICE— MANHATTAN—LATE AFTERNOON

The office is in great commotion. People scurry about with color swipes, fabric books, samples, tear sheets, and other fashion-related paraphernalia. DOLLY through the action to find a small group of people huddled around Spring's massive Louis XIV desk.

SPRING'S voice bellows from within the group.

SPRING

Quiet, please!

*All goes silent. A thin trail of cigarette smoke snakes upward, form-
ing a large cloud that hovers over their heads. PUSH THROUGH the
group to reveal Spring Sommer seated behind her desk, surrounded by
her most trusted associates: MICK, BROOKE, MALCOLM, and
IAN. A diamond-encrusted cigarette holder extends from between her
high-gloss fingertips, a smoldering cigarette at its end. The group
waits breathlessly as Spring slowly flips through a large loose-leaf
book dummy filled with photographs, fabrics, and color swatches, then
carefully closes the book. We can now read the cover.*

*HAUTELAW, INC.
NEW YORK, NY
AUTUMN/WINTER TRENDS REPORT*

SPRING (cont.)

FAABULOUS! Oscar will be simply awestruck!
It's the most brilliant piece of style reportage
I've ever seen! A work of sheer genius!
Mick, daaahling, how ever did you do it?

MICK

Well, to be honest, Spring, without Imogene's
superhuman style sense, none of this would
have been possible.

SPRING

Imogene! Of course!

The group parts to reveal Imogene, looking completely radiant in her
Stella McCartney superhero cape. A roar of applause ensues as she
steps forward demurely, everyone gazing at her with expressions of
deepest admiration and fondness.

CLOSE ON BROOKE, who holds back, seething with jealousy. Her
cell phone rings. She looks at the screen, then disappears into the
crowd to answer.

SPRING

What can I say? Your work is remarkable!
Profound! I wouldn't be surprised if there was a Pulitzer
in this!

(sotto voce)

By the way, sweetie, you look smashing.
Who's slimming you this season?

Brooke snaps her phone shut, a cunning smile on her lips.

BROOKE

(interrupts)

That was Oscar's assistant.

A wave of panic races through the group.

BROOKE (con't.)

The schedule has changed.

His helicopter leaves at four thirty. Sharp.

MALCOLM

(alarmed)

It's four twenty now!

SPRING

(with steely determination)

If we don't get this book to him before he leaves

for Kuala Lumpur, we'll lose the account!

BROOKE

(falsely)

I'll bet Imogene can get there in time.

IMOGENE

(stammers)

M-m-me?

SPRING

Of course! Imogene!

IMOGENE

I just don't know. I mean . . .

MICK

You have to do this, Imogene!

The future of Hautelaw is at stake!

Spring holds out a set of keys.

SPRING

Here! Take my car!

And remember, we're all counting on you!

Don't let us down!

Imogene dashes out. CLOSE ON BROOKE, who chuckles madly.

INT. GARAGE — LATE AFTERNOON

CLOSE: A car door opens in blackness — a pair of tight Gucci leather pants slides into seat.

SFX: Leather stretching.

CLOSE: Breasts inflate in skin-tight Gucci leather jacket — à la Lara Croft.

*CLOSE: REARVIEW MIRROR: Lip gloss applied to full, red lips.
VARI-SPEED: Pull out from mirror and swing around to 3/4 of
Imogene. Imogene pulls out cell phones in each hand—drops bat-
tery packs like ammo clips—plugs phones into dual car jacks.*

*CLOSE: Sexy, six-inch Blahnik high-heeled boot
stomps clutch.*

*CLOSE: Chanel-lacquered red nails insert BMW
logo key into ignition.*

*WIDE: Dark garage. The powerful engine turns over and revs. Brake
lights pierce the blackness.*

CLOSE: Red nails jam shift mechanism into gear.

*WIDE: Tires squeal as the polished-to-perfection black BMW Z4 M
convertible tears toward camera backward, swings into 180-degree
turn, and races away.*

EXT. GARMENT DISTRICT, 38TH STREET—LATE AFTERNOON

*WIDE: busy, wet, New York street. The Z4 flies out from garage
ramp, briefly airborne, turns into traffic, and rockets past camera.
Pedestrians remain unaware. The Z4 races through crowded streets,
weaving through a maze of trucks and cabs. Ahead, men pushing
racks of designer clothing cross the street directly in front of us.*

C.U. TACHOMETER: The needle jumps as engine guns.

WIDE: Men see car coming and madly push clothing racks across the street, parting just in time for Z4 to blow through. Vari-speed to extreme slow-mo as clothes fly up like autumn leaves.

LOW ANGLE: The Z4 blows past camera, makes sharp right onto cross street, and vanishes around corner.

EXT. DA SILVANO RESTAURANT, SIXTH AVENUE — LATE AFTERNOON
WIDE: The Da Silvano sidewalk café tables.

MEDIUM: A waiter blithely exits the restaurant carrying a tray of veal chops to a waiting table.

WIDE: The Z4 speeds up the sidewalk toward the waiter.

CLOSE — WAITER: The Z4 blows past. The waiter looks from Z4 to tray. Veal chops are gone.

WIDE: The Z4 slams to a stop at the end of the sidewalk and backs up to the waiter.

MEDIUM — REAR: Imogene's arm quickly reaches out and snaps up a napkin from the tray — races off again.

EXT. 42ND STREET—LATE AFTERNOON

WIDE—ACROSS STREET: An NYPD cruiser sits quietly, motor running.

EXT.—NYPD CRUISER: A sexy NYPD cop sips from coffee cup and munches on donut.

WIDE—ACROSS STREET: The Z4 zooms past.

MEDIUM—REAR: The cruiser peels out after Z4.

INT. Z4—LATE AFTERNOON

REARVIEW MIRROR: We see the cruiser, lights flashing, weaving through traffic as it closes in on Z4.

CLOSE: Imogene shifts her eyes from mirror and leans into the wheel, smiles ruefully.

CLOSE: Nails jam gearshift.

CLOSE: Boot stomps gas.

EXT. INTERSECTION, MADISON AND 42ND—LATE AFTERNOON

The Z4 careens around corner L-R into oncoming traffic—cruiser close behind.

EXT. MADISON AVE. — LATE AFTERNOON

Z4 and cruiser play cat and mouse through heavy traffic. Other cruisers pull in from side streets and join the chase.

CUT TO:

EXT. HELIPORT — LATE AFTERNOON

LOW ANGLE: Z4 flies over camera and zooms through gate toward waiting helicopter.

MEDIUM: Z4 slams on brakes and does four-wheel drift across wet pavement, stopping next to Oscar de la Renta, who is just stepping into state-of-the-art chopper.

CLOSE: Z4 door opens and long, sexy legs stand.

VARIOUS SHOTS: Police stop dead in their tracks — lean out of car windows, crane over steering wheels, drop jaws, etc., as Imogene bends over into car, reaching for the sample book.

MEDIUM: Imogene hands book to Oscar. Oscar smiles.

> OSCAR
> Hello, Imogene.

> IMOGENE
> Hello, Oscar.

OSCAR

You made it with thirty seconds to spare.

CRANE SHOT: Widen to see fifty police cars, their lights flashing on heliport. A beautiful red-orange sunset bathes the scene as Oscar's chopper lifts off.

FADE OUT

March 19

Fwd: re: IMOGENE PROJECT

Fm: Sheila Hicks <SH@S-H-Entertainment.com>

Subject: Imogene Project

Dear Sheila,

Regretfully, we are passing on your project.

Unfortunately, it wasn't exactly what we had in mind,

despite the inventive costume descriptions.

Best of luck,

Emily Tweed

chapter eight

They Shoot Interns, Don't They?

date: MARCH 17

To: Paolo

From: Imogene

Re: Post-Traumatic Text Syndrome!

I miss you . . . sooooooooooo much!!! To answer your question, the rejection from Twin Tweed definitely stung, but I guess I'll live. Sheila says it's no biggie, because she already has another meeting set up for me.

P.S. She said you can send her your reel!

entered the room with Evie in tow. A woman with short yellow hair and a headset sat behind a large Brazilian rosewood reception desk reading a screenplay. Behind her, tiers of shelves were stacked with scripts, many of them swathed in the signature black covers of S-H-E (Sheila Hicks Entertainment), clearly connoting ownership and position in the Hollywood hierarchy. In fact, it was because of Sheila that I was here at all, in über-director Ira Spellman's studio bungalow. He was midshoot on what was rumored to be *the* most expensive remake in Hollywood history.

"Excuse me."

The receptionist lifted her eyes and studied me.

"I'm here to see Mr. Spellman," I said cheerfully. "Sheila Hicks sent me."

She closed her script and immediately punched a button on the switchboard.

"Un-reee-al!" Evie mouthed, suppressing her excitement.

Thankfully, for the most part, Evie seemed her old self again. After the Tina Lorenz show, she had been steaming mad. I knew I had to conjure up something really big to make it up to her. Luckily, I managed to get Evie on the visitor's list, and her heart, which had been suspended in Arctic ice, melted, just like that.

I had convinced Sheila that she was a much-needed part of my support group, along with Toy, of course. Which was true . . . well, partly anyway. I mean, I really *was* utterly nervous about the whole Spellman thing.

The receptionist nodded toward an enormous rotunda waiting area centered beneath a vast, domed skylight and said that Mr. Spellman's assistant would be with us shortly.

We followed the path of deep blue and yellow Mexican tiles that led us there. At the rotunda's center was an extravagant indoor rain forest, replete with lush foliage, delicate waterfall (mist included), and vibrantly colored tropical birds. It was magical. Clearly no expense had been spared.

Evie stepped toward the waterfall. Something had caught her eye.

"Girlena! You've got to see this!"

I crouched down next to her and peered into the rain forest. There, perched on the rocks beneath the waterfall, was a tiny, bright blue frog. Under normal circumstances I would have leaped back and said something like "Ewwww!" But this frog was absolutely adorable.

"Isn't it just the cutest thing you've ever seen?" Evie gushed. "Maybe if you give it a kiss it will turn into a prince."

"Oh, Evie, don't be silly." I giggl=ed.

"Go on, girlena. It might be good luck."

"A girl could always use a bit of good luck," I murmured. So I decided to humor Evie (and myself) with a pretend kiss.

I leaned forward and closed my eyes, when suddenly an electrifying *ZAP* sound pierced the air. The jungle disappeared. Completely. What was left was a face. It was Dustin's face.

Evie's startled scream made me lose my balance, and I fell into the face. Our lips pressed together in an accidental kiss. I pushed away with a gasp and stood bolt upright, in a state of firsthand embarrassment.

"Are you all right?" he asked, concerned.

"Not sure yet," I replied, heart pounding. I mean, I couldn't tell who was more shocked: Evie, who just stood there with her eyes bugging out; me; or Dustin.

"Imogene," he said. "Well, if this isn't my lucky day. Though the last place I'd have thought we'd meet again was at a hologram test in the Spellman bungalow." He smiled that broad, radiant smile. I nearly melted.

Evie, meanwhile, was gaping, not at Dustin but at the guy standing beside Dustin with a laptop and a box of wires in his hands. The techie boy fumbled with his gadgets, clearly not knowing what to make of any of this.

"How rude of me. Marcus, meet the lovely Imogene," Dustin said. Then he turned toward Evie. "And this is Evie, if memory serves."

Evie continued gazing at Marcus. Marcus gazed back.

I was still confused. "What happened to the rain forest? And what were you doing?"

"I believe I was kissing you," he said. I could feel a major (Chanel "Enchanteresse") blush blooming on my cheekbones.

"It was the frog I was kissing," I corrected demurely.

"I'll let you in on a little secret," Dustin whispered sweetly. "It's not only in fairy tales that frogs turn out to be princes."

Oh . . . he is so beautiful!

"We were conducting a hologram test," Marcus said, breaking the spell.

"Marcus here is Spellman's special effects expert," Dustin explained. "We were just testing out a project I hope to be intimately involved with in the future. It's a pretty cool special effect—but not as pretty, cool, or special as you, Imogene," he added with a corny wink.

The blush was off the charts.

To change the subject, I shifted focus to Marcus. Turns out Spellman had hired him as the visual effects wizard for a virtual theme park ride idea he was toying with, hence the hologram. Judging from the results, Marcus was definitely on the right track.

"It looks like I'll need to run some diagnostics on the AI," Marcus said as he flipped open a black laptop. A cluster of wires streamed out of its side and onto the floor of the rotunda. Recessed in the ceiling was a series of tiny holographic projectors.

"Some of the frogs have been acting up lately," Marcus said, not taking his eyes off of Evie.

Dustin smiled mischievously, flashing his now familiar sunbeam of a smile. "Naughty frogs."

"I guess the program's still a little buggy," Marcus said. Evie blinked, still locked into a visual trance. Dustin and I looked at her and Marcus. Marcus seemed completely smitten. By the same token, Evie hadn't taken her eyes off Marcus since he appeared. I could smell the wood burning inside her brain as it thought, *He's so hot. I love techie boys. Girlena, can I just stay here forever while you go off to your meeting?*

But being around Dustin like this was getting dangerous for me—I couldn't risk leaving Evie and finding myself alone with him.

"Evie and I have to go now, don't we, Evie?"

Evie and Marcus were still in deep stare.

"Do we?" Evie said dreamily.

Evie might have been tuned out, but Dustin picked up on my urge to flee. "This is the second time you've run away from me. If I didn't know better," he said, "I'd say you don't like me, Imogene."

"No, really, we've got to be going now. Don't we, Evie?"

"No."

Thankfully—I say thankfully because I had now become keenly aware of how attracted I was becoming to Dustin and how bad, bad, bad that could be—it wasn't long before a woman in a dark pin-striped suit appeared.

"Hi, I'm Meg, Mr. Spellman's assistant. I'm sorry, but Mr. Spellman's had a last-minute schedule change and is shooting through lunch. Would you mind meeting him on the set instead?"

I couldn't believe it. We were actually going to watch Ira Spellman shoot a movie! Better yet, I was going to talk to Ira Spellman about shooting *my movie*!

"Sure," I replied, hardly breathing.

Meg produced a photocopied map.

"You'll meet with Mr. Spellman here," she said, pointing to an area indicating an enormous soundstage. "Follow the road all the way past the lake to Stage Twenty-nine."

"What movie are they shooting?" Evie asked, finally taking her eyes off Tech Boy.

"A remake. That's all I can tell you."

Her cell phone rang. "You better run. I wrote my number on the map," she said. "Call me if you get lost."

Dustin gestured at Marcus, who was still looking at Evie, completely gaga. "We'd be happy to escort you there," Dustin offered.

"That's all right," I said quickly, as Evie shot me a pleading glare. "We'll find our way just fine."

The first AD (assistant director) stared at his watch so hard I thought it was going to melt. "We break in five," he snapped. "Have a seat."

For the uninitiated, one o'clock is the official lunch hour in L.A. You won't find an agent alive in their office at that hour. And when they go out, so do the directors, writers, producers, actors, and anyone else in the top tier of the studio food chain. That is not to say they're not hard at work. On the contrary! They may be out of the office, but they're still busy, pounding BlackBerrys and cell phones, calling New York, and making the deals that keep the movie machine running smoothly year in and year out.

Men clearly possess an uncanny knack for ESP because the first thing we did after leaving the bungalow was get lost. Not that it was intentional or anything, because it wasn't, but we did manage to lose our way somewhere between Rome and Flatbush. Evie kept taking little side trips to check out the different movies being made. Fortunately, we ran into some Confederate Army extras heading toward Atlanta. When we heard the word "Spellman" mumbled, we figured we would follow them.

We plunked ourselves down and stared breathlessly at the scenario before us—the city of Atlanta during the Civil War, with all the grit, smoke, and costumes exactly as they were then. I mean, the set was so completely brilliant that we had to keep pinching ourselves to make sure it wasn't a dream.

Horses and their handlers, carriages, and cannons moved in a double-speed ballet of ordered chaos. In the center of it all, a cluster of people huddled around a single man whose only job appeared to be wandering around the set, making comments on everything within view. He was short and stocky with dark-rimmed glasses, caterpillar eyebrows, and wavy hair—hair he ran his fingers through whenever someone asked him a question, which appeared to be continuously. When he wasn't running his fingers through his hair, he spent his time in bouts of reflection (in which he would fold his arms, stare at the ground, and rub his chin) and bouts of complete abandon (in which he would wave his arms about wildly and yell at no one in particular, walking so rapidly that the "huddle" would literally have to jog after him to hear what he was saying. Needless to say, this was the one and only Ira Spellman.

The first AD broke from the huddle, bullhorn in hand, and clambered onto some nearby hay bales. "Lunch! One hour!" he shouted.

"OMG! How insane! I just realized what movie this is!" Evie whispered.

"Really?"

"It's *Gone with the Wind*!"

A young woman in a headset and clipboard appeared next to us. "Which one of you is Imogene?" she asked.

"That's me."

"Mr. Spellman can see you now."

I took Evie's hand and squeezed it. "I'll be back in a few. *Do not go anywhere*," I warned.

"Don't worry, girlena! Where would I possibly go?"

Rather than dwell on the obvious, I gave her hand another squeeze, checked my lip gloss (aka instant sparkle and shine), and followed clipboard girl. Spellman was alone, slowly pacing down the middle of the main street, scrutinizing everything in sight.

"Mr. Spellman?" said clipboard girl. "This is Imogene." She hovered for a moment, waiting for possible instructions, then disappeared.

He fired off his opening volley — "So what do you think?" — indicating the surrounding set. He was one of those people who speaks in rapid bursts. "Atlanta, 1868. Down to the last hand-forged nail. Cost me twenty million."

"Incredible," I said.

"Yes, it is. In the original they burned down the entire set for this scene, but these days I can do everything digitally. Not a single flame anywhere. And it looks *better* than real. Not to mention all the money I save the studio."

He stopped and watched a couple of prop men loading an old wagon with supplies.

"Are those bananas?" Spellman barked, pointing at a

bunch of fake bananas behind a fake sack of flour. "Because the Confederacy didn't have any bananas."

Ooh, a fellow trend spotter. Anyone who can call out a fake is all right in my book. Personally, I pride myself on spotting fakes a mile away: face-lift, nose job, toupée, dye job. Though I must admit, it's hard to ascribe any real value to such talents.

"Right, Mr. Spellman," one of them replied, quickly removing the bananas.

Spellman moved on. "So you're the Hautelaw Girl. I saw you on television the other night. Sheila didn't tell me you were a friend of Beyoncé's."

"Actually, we're just —"

"Your story's got potential. Young girl in Paris for the first time gets involved with jewel smugglers. Falls in love with the gang leader."

"What? But that's not what happened."

A woman stepped up to him and held out several pages of pink paper. "Scene 343 revisions."

"What about 270? I need 270."

"On the way."

Spellman folded the pages and shoved them into his back pocket without losing a step.

"What's the difference?" he continued. "It's all fiction. The story just needs a little embellishment."

"But Paris really happened."

"Sure it did. Look, I know what Sheila pitched me, but what girl goes to Paris and discovers a misanthropic fashion designer while uncovering a smuggling ring? Who's going to believe that?"

I had to admit, when he put it that way it did sound a little far-fetched.

An actress in period dress ran up to him, holding a well-thumbed script.

"Ira," she panted, "I don't understand this scene. I'm running out of the building when the troops arrive, but why? What's my motivation?"

"Your sweetheart lost his leg at Appomattox. He was a dancer."

"How tragic! Thank you!" And with that she was gone.

"It may be your life story, but it's not going to sell. Trust me, I know movies and I know what people like, and these days people like suspense movies."

"Suspense?"

"I'm thinking this girl goes to Paris and gets trained by her boyfriend to become a master jewel thief to help support her impoverished parents back home—you know, good girl-gone-bad-with-a-heart-of-gold sort of thing . . ."

He was back to his version of my story. "On her first solo job she steals the priceless Persimmon Diamond from a billionaire playboy, who catches her in the act but is so taken with her cunning and beauty he lets her go. In the end she has to choose between the billionaire and the jewel thief."

Okay, maybe he *was* onto something.

At that moment clipboard girl returned. "You're needed on the set, Mr. Spellman."

Spellman nodded, then turned back toward me. "Send

me some pages in a couple of days." He squeezed my shoulder and walked away. And that was it, end of meeting.

With my head still swirling with enormous diamonds and gorgeous billionaires, I went back to find Evie. Of course, she was nowhere to be found; nor was her cell phone picking up. I wandered around the lot until I stumbled across a large trailer with red block letters on its side that read ADRIANNA HEATH / COSTUME DESIGN.

OMG—I knew it!

"Can you believe this?" Evie squealed in ecstasy, twirling around inside the wardrobe trailer. She had on a white crinoline skirt with a champagne and cream Charles Worth-esque overskirt. Definitely not of the époque, but gorgeous nonetheless.

I pulled the door shut behind me.

"Evie! What are you doing in here?"

The trailer was lined with tier after tier of costumes, one on top of the other. It was like being in the ultimate closet! Only this one was filled with unbelievable outfits, every bit the quality of couture.

"It's my karma, girlena! Fate put Adrianna Heath's trailer in my path. I mean, *look* at this stuff!!"

Evie pulled down a powder blue silk bustle gown. "You've *got* to try this on!"

"No! We're not supposed to be in here, Evie, let alone try things on!"

"Just ask yourself one question, okay? 'When will I ever, *ever* get the opportunity to wear something like this again?'"

She had a point there. It's not every day that a girl like *moi* gets the opportunity to wear an Adrianna Heath original.

"Besides," Evie continued, "everyone's out to lunch!"

"Only this once," I said firmly. "And then we go!"

"But how am I going to meet Adrianna Heath if I leave?"

"Look, I'll ask Sheila if she'll do an introduction. Okay? It's much better than ambushing her in her trailer, believe me."

"Promise?"

"Promise."

We spent the next ten minutes flitting about the trailer in costumed bliss trying on this and that. Not to be denied the full effect, we put on wigs, shoes, and gloves, channeling as much Southern belle-icousness as possible. Unfortunately, like most euphoria, ours was short-lived. The door burst open and standing there, bullhorn in hand, was the first AD.

"Hey, didn't you hear me?" he shouted. "Lunch is over. We're back on set!"

Okay, this is the kind of stuff that always, I mean, *always* gets me into trouble. I mean, rather than risk any firsthand embarrassment by revealing my true identity and making some feeble, albeit innocent excuse about being unable to resist the whims of my BFF, not to mention the risk of being dragged before Ira Spellman and unceremoniously thrown off the set, which could put an end to any present and or future movie deal that might possibly come to pass, I elected to go with the flow.

"We had a last-minute change of clothes," I said, hoping that between the old "you're annoying me" routine and the wigs we wouldn't be recognized.

"When did that happen?" he said, glaring at us suspiciously.

I shrugged my shoulders.

"Why is it always the extras?" he grumbled. "All right, you two, let's go!"

We followed him back to the set, where we were handed off to the second AD, who wrangled us behind the doorway of a building along with a burly guy in overalls named Pete, who turned out to be a stuntman, and an adorable little girl named Sasha, who threatened us with bodily harm if we hogged the scene. According to the second AD, all we had to do was dash out of the building "on cue," make a right at the barrels, and pretend to run for our lives down the street—it was acting, after all. I mean, don't get me wrong, under normal circumstances the chance to be an extra in a Spellman movie, or any movie for that matter, would have been truly exciting—it's the kind of experience you tell your grandchildren about. But this was over the top. Way over. My fears of being recognized by Spellman completely overshadowed any future entertainment value. Evie, on the other hand, was pumped. I looked at her and shook my head.

"Of all the things we've ever done," I mumbled, "this is, by far, the craziest."

"I know," she replied, beaming. "It's brilliant."

The AD's radio chirped into action.

"Okay, everyone!" he announced. "Get ready!"

I yanked my wig down tight and pushed the bangs in front of my face. Through a doorway I watched as Spellman climbed onto a crane platform and slowly rose up in the air. When the crane stopped moving, Spellman raised a bullhorn to his lips and hollered, "Action!"

I kept my head down for fear of being recognized and

plunged out into the street, with all the other extras. Sasha first, of course.

The problem was that nobody said anything about there being explosions everywhere, not to mention massive banks of blinding lights, and smoke, and horses running wild, and people screaming. I mean, somewhere between almost being run down by a pumpkin wagon and looking up and seeing stuntman Pete soar overhead in a cloud of fiery smoke, my "mock panic" turned into "genuine terror." Forget about being recognized, I bolted down the street, flailing my arms and screaming for help (which everyone assumed was acting), only to be enveloped in a cloud of thick black smoke. I glanced over my shoulder, hoping to catch sight of Evie, but instead, as the smoke cleared, the caterpillar eyebrows of Ira Spellman were there, floating about three feet behind me on the crane—the gigantic eye of a lens pointing right in my face.

"Arrrrgghhhhhhh!" I screamed.

"Brilliant!" he shouted.

I was now in a blind frenzy, running as fast as I could to get away from Spellman, who hovered behind me, shouting directions—as if I could do anything other than run and scream. In fact, I was so busy trying to get away from him I didn't see the mud puddle in front of me, which I literally dove into, eliciting a "Stupendous!" from Spellman as he and his crane moved on to other fodder. By then all I wanted to do was drown, which I probably would have had it not been for Evie, who yanked me out of the muck under cover of smoke and cannon fire. She didn't look much better than I did.

"C'mon!" she hollered. "Now's our chance!"

We hobbled down a narrow alley past some hay bales and gobs of electrical cables. In my exhausted stupor I stumbled over a cable, causing a loud electrical "pop" sound somewhere behind me. I was too limp to turn around and see what it was, but by the time we reached the craft service table, plumes of smoke were rising over the set. Convinced that I had accidentally set fire to Atlanta, I made up my mind to confess my crime to anybody and everybody who would listen, starting with craft services. But when I looked back at the set and saw, rising through the smoke and flames, Ira Spellman, soaring over the melee like some great, hairy bird, gleefully barking orders at his camera crew to "Shoot, shoot, shoot!" I didn't feel as bad. In fact, I felt downright exhilarated.

As Evie and I quietly made our getaway, to the sound of approaching fire engines, I began to realize that the one simple truth beneath all of my fear, and nervousness, and insecurity, was the realization that more than ever, I wanted to succeed in this weird and wonderful world called Hollywood very, very badly.

chapter nine

To Catch a Thief

❄   ❄   ❄

EXT. BUILDING — NIGHT

Dressed in a black stretch Azzedine Alaia catsuit, HAUTELAW GIRL rifles through her gear: night-vision goggles, rope, carabiners, belays, motion detector, subsonic audio encryption device, digital wrist camera, lip gloss. She casually glances over her shoulder, hair falling sideways. Camera pulls back. She is suspended high above the ground, dangling beside the window of a gorgeous Parisian townhouse. Below her, an elegant garden party is in full swing. A perfect hole is cut in the glass—clearly she's been busy. CLOSE UP. She reaches through the hole and with a quiet click, she's in.

INT. LIBRARY — NIGHT

The library is a miniature museum, filled with rare books, paintings,

106

and priceless works of art. HAUTELAW GIRL moves silently through the room. Lenses of her night-vision goggles glow a soft opalescent green like the eyes of a cat. She bypasses several master-pieces and heads for the bookshelves. Quickly scans row after row with laser-focused intensity. A set of leather-bound folios sandwiched between lion's-head bookends catches her attention. She slides her gloved hand across the volumes and stops on the bookend. She hesitates a moment, then carefully pulls it out, sets it on a nearby table, and deftly runs her fingers over it. She presses something on the back of the mane and with a soft pop, *the head of the lion flips back, revealing a pale, reddish-orange diamond the size of a walnut.*

HAUTELAW GIRL lowers her goggles and holds the diamond up to the moonlight.

HAUTLAW GIRL
(whispers)
Magnificent.

Suddenly the deep, sensual voice of AUGUSTIN speaks behind her.

AUGUSTIN (V. O.)
I knew you would come.

HAUTELAW GIRL slowly turns and smiles faintly.

HAUTELAW GIRL
Really.

AUGUSTIN

No one can resist the Persimmon Diamond.

AUGUSTIN flips on a small lamp, revealing his irresistibly sexy figure — tall, dark, Armani-ed.

AUGUSTIN (Cont.)

Especially a beautiful woman like you.

HAUTELAW GIRL nods her thanks.

AUGUSTIN (Cont.)

But tell me, how did you know where to find
it? You didn't even look in the safe.

HAUTELAW GIRL

Easy. The only place to hide a priceless
object among priceless objects is in plain sight.
I simply looked for the least valuable thing in the room.

AUGUSTIN steps closer, drawn to her.

HAUTELAW GIRL (Cont.)

Of course, having it support a rare first edition
folio set of *Hung Lo's Exotic Fruit of the Far East* was helpful.

AUGUSTIN

Brains and beauty. But not as clever as you
think. The bookend has a silent alarm system.

HAUTELAW GIRL
I know.

AUGUSTIN is stunned, speechless.

HAUTELAW GIRL
I wanted to see you one last time.

AUGUSTN
You could have called. Sent me a text message.

HAUTELAW GIRL
You know the police suspect me.
And you have the foundation to think of—
all those people who depend on you every day.
I won't let you put them at risk for my sake.

AUGUSTIN
I don't care. I love you, Hautelaw Girl.

HAUTELAW GIRL
This is good-bye, Augustin.

*In the distance, SIRENS are heard. HAUTELAW GIRL slips a leg
out the window and holds up the diamond.*

HAUTELAW GIRL (Cont.)
I'll keep this for old times' sake.

AUGUSTIN runs to the window, but she is gone. He leans out into the night, his eyes red, his rugged features convulsed with emotion.

AUGUSTIN

(sotto voce)

Adieu, ma chérie. Adieu.

FADE OUT

Date: March 20

To: Sheila Hicks

CC: Imogene

Re: The Imogene Project

Thank you for thinking of us for Imogene.

Unfortunately, after carefully reviewing the sample script pages, Mr. Spellman has decided to pass on the project. In his words: "It's not my cup of tea."

Good luck to Imogene with all her future endeavors.

Meg C.

Spellman Entertainment

chapter ten

Saturday Night Fever

Hey Imogene,

Some friends are throwing a little soiree at Oblivion
and would simply love to meet you—or should I say,
Hautelaw Girl.

Sorry, no BFFs.

Saturday, 11:00 p.m.

Toodles!

xoxo Mia

✳   ✳   ✳

W hen it comes to clubs, super best friends (SBFFs)
are like the Mafia—if you have one, you're *made*.
Fortunately for me, I now had Mia. Which is

how I managed to breeze into Oblivion, the hottest mobile club in L.A.

Only insiders know its location. It changes from week to week. At the ungodly hour others would turn into pumpkins, party people are, without even batting a faux eyelash, just coming out to play. Lucky for me, tonight Oblivion was just up the road in Malibu.

I navigated my way through the mass of undulating bodies as waves of neon blue and purple lasers swept over the crowd with alien precision. On the far side, luxurious banquettes rested discreetly beneath a broad crescent of copper palm trees, their gleaming aluminum fronds arcing forward over the dance floor. A second story, filled with plush chairs and intimate tables, bowed outward, its railing crowded with the silhouettes of people watching the energized flux below with casual indifference.

"Mia, hi," I said, finding her at an upper-level table scattered with candy jelly shots and pink champagne sorbets. She wore a highlighter yellow, asymmetrical silk dress and a pair of strappy sandals; the Juliet ribbons decorating her high, makeshift updo added to her goddess vibe.

"I'm so glad you could make it. Sorry about not inviting your . . . *unusual* BFF." She smiled disingenuously and paused, searching for a qualifier. "I just thought we'd be able to get to know each other better without her—just this once."

At this I felt a stab of guilt. Okay, confession time, I had let my inner wimpitude prevail and ditched Evie for the night. I know I'm a rat. A big fat rat! I mean, so what if Evie was *unusual*, even downright odd—she was still my best friend. But Mia's invitation was impossible to resist—Lord knows I tried. I did! But Evie was totally engrossed in our latest fashion week challenge, and she'd made it clear from her grumbling that my non-FFC-focused interruptions were only getting in her way. I'm sure I could have convinced her to come along had I only told her where I was going, but the truth is, a small part of me *wanted* to go without her. After the Spellman-set incident, I was the teensiest bit wary of bringing Evie on any other Tinseltown outings. She just doesn't fit into that world the way I do. And I guess for the first time in my life, I wanted to experience something without her. You know, have a life that was just about me, that didn't include someone who got me into trouble every time I turned around.

I mean, what if I *had* been caught by Spellman? My would-be career would be over before it even got off the ground, all thanks to Evie and her brilliant knack for trouble. For the first time in my life, the spotlight was on me. Just me. And with a simple e-mail, Mia had fired an arrow into my Achilles heel, tapping my one fatal flaw, my "I hope you like me" syndrome, by which I couldn't help wanting Mia to find me, Imogene, worthy. So I lied to Evie, telling her I was going to spend a few hours catching up with Paolo over the phone, and that she shouldn't wait up for my return.

"Evie's not so bad," I fumbled weakly. "If only you knew her better."

"Right," said Mia flatly.

"Imogene," Ashlie, Mia's attention-starved sidekick, greeted me. "Ohmigod, we saw you at the Tina Lorenz show

113

on the news. You looked so fabulous!" I guess when you're number two you really do try harder. "We didn't know you were friends with Beyoncé!"

After the accolades, Mia introduced me to the rest of her posse—alpha daughters and sons of the rich and famous. Austin, son of a seventies rock star legend; Sari, daughter of a notable novelist; Chesley, stepdaughter of an exalted real estate agent; and Duff, son of a biggie music exec. And they didn't waste any time letting me in on their secrets, either. Within twenty minutes I knew the most intimate details of their lives—highlights and lowlights.

A new song started blasting, and a gaggle of girls squealed with delight as they rushed downstairs to the karaoke lounge. "We're going to be rock stars!"

Mia rolled her eyes and said, "Thank Gawd they're gone! This is supposed to be an exclusive venue, not a dweeb convention."

Everyone had a good chuckle and headed to the dance floor, leaving Mia and me alone. "Don't mind them," she said. "They're only here because I need a designated driver."

She sidled a bit closer. "So, *Hautelaw Girl*, now that I have you all to myself, you must tell me everything."

"Everything?" I repeated.

"Look, if we're going to be friends, I need to know everything about you."

"Mia, please. Look at you—your life is a thousand times more interesting than mine."

She laughed at this.

"You'd be surprised. I'm not that interesting at all.

Besides, there's already a glut of L.A. heir-head party girl stories on the market. Paris has had that one locked up for ages."

I must have spent an hour talking about life as Hautelaw Girl, and Mia was a great listener. She barely blinked the whole time. I was right in the middle of the steamiest scene from my trip to Paris when something flashed.

"Who's your new friend, Mia?" a voice behind a huge lens asked.

Mia put her arm around me and beamed her best media smile.

"This is my new BFF, Hautelaw Girl."

Someone shouted, "Hey, it's Hautelaw Girl!" and we were instantly swarmed by paparazzi.

"What's it like to be Hautelaw Girl? Are you here to make a movie? Who are you hooking up with?"

Mia leaned over and whispered, "I'll be back later. Don't

worry, you'll get used to it. It's part of your life now . . . like breathing."

But she was wrong, I didn't need to get used to it. I loved it! I could feel the rush of adrenaline pulsing through me like fire. And the more the flashes went off, the more powerful the feeling grew. It *was* a drug.

Someone shouted something downstairs and the mob of paparazzi vanished, hot on the trail of another celebrity, no doubt. I looked around, and Mia was gone too.

I picked up my glass and wandered into a small side room. It was dark, with only a few couples quietly kissing. Behind the bar, a flat-screen monitor broadcast the local news. I dropped into a chair and watched. They were wrapping up the week's events—you know, police chases, political scandals, and celebrity gossip. The screen then flipped to a shot of a reporter who stood, microphone in hand, in front of a studio gate. He was going on about the sudden blaze that had swept through the Spellman movie set. The story was cut with various shots of fire trucks and smoke billowing from a distant unknown back lot. A chill ran down my spine. I slid my sunglasses on and slunk down in my seat.

"Can you believe that?" someone said, slipping into the seat beside me. A whiff of Vetiver, my current favorite opposite sex scent du jour, tickled my nose. It was Dustin! He must have appeared while I was busy trying to be invisible. I mentally recorded his demeanor: *intelligent, happy, bold, unabashedly sure of himself, but without a trace of conceit.* It was a nice combination.

"Rumor is, a couple of outsiders snuck onto the set

pretending to be extras and somehow started the fire."

He looked at me sideways. No, I thought, he couldn't possibly *know*. Suspect . . . maybe.

"Pathetic what some people will do to be in the movies. Sad, really."

He held my shaded eyes with his gaze. I simply couldn't turn away. Once again I was stunned by how gorgeous he was . . . and how mature. I mean, he couldn't have been more than a couple of years older than me, but he was already a man. I was still traversing Teenager 101.

Dustin was rapidly becoming well known around Hollywood, B movies aside. Despite that, he was not to be found in the gossip columns—I know, I checked. What I *did* find out was that he was on everyone's soon-to-be hot list, including Sheila's. And was considered one of the better actors around town. But in spite of all his looks and talent, he was still waiting for his big break. I was completely sympathetic. I mean, nobody knows better than me what it's like to toil and struggle and try to keep your dream alive.

After a few silent moments passed, I finally managed a "What are you doing here?"

He shook his head. "You never called, so I came looking for you."

"It's not like I haven't seen you recently." I laughed.

"The problem is, you haven't seen *nearly* enough of me. So I came to rescue you."

"From what?"

"Paparazzi . . . all these phony-baloney people . . . yourself maybe."

"I wasn't aware I needed rescuing."

His eyes flashed in the darkness. "Did you know that right outside the place you're sitting is one of the most beautiful beaches on the coast? Perfect for a nice, quiet walk. Full moon, sand between your toes—could be nice."

I've always had a weak spot for a knight in shining armor. And at that point I'd have gone anywhere with anyone, just to get away from the television news report.

With drinks in hand, we climbed down the small stairway to the beach. A spray of stars shimmered overhead. Couples walked along the sand, enjoying the cool evening air before bedtime. A sudden gust sent a Frisbee off course. Dustin snatched it from the air and held it out to a soaking-wet Labrador that came bounding up; he pretended to throw it, then hid it behind his back. Dustin tossed the Frisbee into the surf and casually turned to me with a slight tilt of his head.

I took my shoes off, scrunching the cool sand between my toes, and let him lead the way.

We found a spot to sit, not too far away from civilization, just far enough.

If only he hadn't opened his mouth, it would have been perfect.

"While I have you all to myself, it wouldn't be crude of me to pick your brain about Paolo, would it?" Dustin asked, explaining that the more he knew, the easier it would be to understand the character when the time came.

I nodded my approval, and Dustin began the questioning. He was beyond curious to know how Paolo dressed, what he liked to do, what his favorite snack was, all the little things that on the outside made Paolo . . . *Paolo*.

I told him about Paolo's addiction to soccer and his *wild* obsession with cars, especially fast Italian ones, and how he is ticklish behind his ears, and that his favorite food is gnocchi.

Sadly, the more I talked about Paolo, the more all the little things that make him so dear to me made me miss him terribly. The fact that we were in constant communication — texting each other several times a day — didn't matter; it just wasn't the same as being with him.

After a bit of introspection, Dustin's expression became serious.

"Is Paolo . . ." Dustin began, but his voice trailed off as he searched for the right word. "Romantic?"

I wasn't sure if it was the way he said it or the way he looked at me, or just the word "romantic." All I knew was that it felt as though a million butterflies were suddenly unleashed in my stomach. My heart sped up, and I could feel the heat in my cheeks as a newborn flush emerged. I was unclear if my blush was because of my love for Paolo — the very thought of him setting off a wave of longing — or if it was caused by my undeniable attraction to Dustin.

"I . . . I guess so, yes," I stammered, praying that he wouldn't sense my attraction.

I shoved my hand inside my bag and grappled for my obsession du jour — "paparazzi pink" lip gloss. It was useless. Dustin moved closer. I felt a rush of heat radiating from his crystalline skin. It was beyond overwhelming. So strong was his magnetism that I could feel my natural defense system melting away by the second.

I had to do something QUICK—but what?

I shut my eyes and started counting. *If I count up to ten, he'll stop looking so drop-dead sexy and . . . One, two, three—by the time I hit twenty he will have gone away . . . OMG—twenty!*

I opened my eyes, hoping and at the same time not hoping that he wouldn't be there. But he was. I shut them again. This time I didn't resist. I couldn't. I let his sweet, intoxicating essence prevail over my senses. He leaned into me with a sensuality as intense as an atomic bomb concentrated down to the size of bouillon cube. Volts of pure electricity shot down my spine as he kissed me.

I curled my toes into the sand once more—this time it was an involuntary reflex. Dustin grilling me about Paolo . . . then kissing me . . . what could it mean? I tried to remember the millions of magazine articles I've read on the subject of deciphering kisses.

kiss on the hand: I adore you
kiss on the cheek: We're friends
kiss on the ear: I'm feeling frisky
kiss on the neck: We belong together
kiss on the shoulder: I want you
French kiss: I want you . . . NOW!

Somehow my rational thoughts and my irrational emotions got jumbled all together like Silly String. All I could do was give in to the kiss and float precariously near the point of no return. Luckily a rogue conscience cell hit its receptor in my brain midkiss, and the fog began to clear. I pushed both my arms firmly against Dustin's strong shoulders.

"I can't . . . I have to go," I said, standing despite an overwhelming desire to stay. Somehow I managed to throw my bag over my shoulder and turn away, averting my eyes. I knew if they'd locked with his, my will would have turned traitor on me. And I shudder to think what would happen then.

I took an initial step forward, and then another, toward the parking lot.

"Imogene . . . please . . . don't go," his soft voice pleaded. I didn't turn around. I couldn't. I didn't want him to see the tears welling up. I just kept on going and going, until I was gone.

chapter eleven

The Big Chill

date: MARCH 21

To: Anyone who'll listen
From: Moi, Imogene
Re: Trend Death Watch:
    1. Miu Miu platforms (sigh)
    2. My reputation (wheeze!)

❋   ❋   ❋

It's a known fact that I am a big believer in the age-old art of letter writing. That's not to say I don't love e-mail, or that I don't simply live to text, but they just don't have the same touchy-feely-ness as a packet of good old-fashioned stationery. You know, the kind for writing long, thoughtful letters home on.

Unfortunately, I was suffering from an extreme case of self-loathing! And rather than force myself to be the faithful (oh, why did I have to use that word?!) correspondent that

I usually am, I had chosen instead to be the very model of a corpse in mid-decomposition, outwardly staring at the ceiling while inwardly pondering the worlds of matter (Toy, fashion, petit fours) and antimatter (knockoff bags, things that smell bad, Brooke). The resulting decision led me to rot in bed to mull over the tenuous status of my karma in light of sneaking out to parties behind BFF's back, being consistently late for FFC, and return flirting and more than two French kisses, constituting out-and-out cheating on my dear, sweet, and hopelessly absent boyfriend.

In short, I was feeling more basket case than girl. I offer as proof of my debilitation the following attempted e-mail response to my mom:

> Dear Mom,
> Having loads of fun at Fashion Fantasy Camp.
> Love to Dad.
> Heart,
> Imogene
> P.S. Say hi to my Vespa
> for me, and don't forget to
> pet my American Express card.

Unfortunately, I was in the fifteen words or less checkout line (postscript not included). That's about all I was capable of. That realization only added fuel to my growing ethical and philosophical doldrums, aka the gloomies. Add to that the fact that my lips were raw and puffy, completely sans moisture—blah! I bit them, ran my fingers over them, and finally plunged my hand into my bag, in search of the lip gloss. Where was it? The hand ran over each seam, each corner. Nothing. Zip. Nada. Silent shriek! Lip gloss withdrawal! It could be an omen, portending some cruel, unusual outcome. Jeez! I can really freak myself out! I've got to get a grip!

Before my morbidly blissful state could cause full rigor mortis, or my stabbed-in-the-back BFF could emerge from her unaware slumber, I managed to force myself out of bed, threw on Lord only knows what, and quietly grabbed the baby blue plastic Shutters room key, which was imprinted with the words YOUR KEY TO INSPIRATION. Unfortunately, those words were currently nonapplicable. I dashed out to the beach for some fresh air and early sun.

When I returned, Evie was gone. In her place was the morning newspaper, opened to the gossip section, with a big fat picture of Mia and me, grinning from ear to ear. At that point there really wasn't anything I could do—the cat was out of the bag. And frankly, I was glad.

Okay, I know I should have said something to Evie last night, but the thought of her giving me the *Evie Eye* again had been too much to bear. Is it my fault that I'm popular, that people want to socialize with me and be my friend? Why can't I have other friends beside Evie? Why do I need permission to go out without her? Why shouldn't I broaden my social circle?

I climbed into the shower, hoping to scrub away some anxiety or at the very least soothe my tormented soul. But the only thing I succeeded in doing was making my fingers puckered. The fact is, I dreaded going to that morning's fashion lecture. I mean, facing Evie there would be bad enough. Add to that the fact that I had fallen woefully behind on all things FFC, thanks to an increasing number of commitments in my new life. Granted, there was no denying the importance of lectures on how to spot a fake Birkin, or little fashion facts and trivia like the difference between paillettes and sequins and why and when to choose them, and lots of other relevant stuff like that. It wasn't a choice—I had to go.

By the time I hit the conference room I was late . . . okay, very late. Cory was just wrapping up her Get Up and Glam report. Predictably, Evie was so upset she wouldn't even *look* at me, let alone speak to me. Despite that, I grabbed the seat next to her.

Everyone else in the conference room seemed near giddy with anticipation—this was to be the morning that the teams would be assigned mentors for something-or-other, yet another FFC project I wasn't prepared for. But while the rest of the campers buzzed and laughed and shifted nervously in their seats, Evie and I sat stone still. How were we supposed to work as a team when we weren't even on speaking terms? And that wasn't the only thing that was making my stomach sick. I'd forgotten all about the team mentors until now, but one urgent thought was coursing through my brain's emergency broadcast system: "Please don't let us get Brooke. Please, any mentor but Brooke."

So it was almost a huge relief when we saw our mentor coming toward us and it was not Brooke.

Almost. Actually, being assigned to EKFALT made both Evie and I a tad anxious. You see, we had had a minor run-in with him and his entourage over some seating at the Jock Lord comeback show a while back—nothing serious, I assure you, but we thought he might hold just the tiniest of grudges against us (even though his assistant should have known better than to stick his finger into my bag if he didn't want to get bit. I mean, Toy was only doing his job!).

Eventually, all six feet four inches of the Editor Formerly Known as Andrew Lyford-Tilly sauntered over wearing a floor-length yellow coque-feather coat and wraparound Dior sunglasses. A single canary diamond caressed his pinky and a homburg, several sizes too small for him, rested at a jaunty angle atop his completely hairless head.

"Well, if it isn't Hautelaw Girl," EFKALT said with a derisive sniff. "Come to grace us with your presence?"

"I'm sorry, I—"

"If I wanted your life story," he interrupted, "I'd read the papers."

Apparently the gossip column was part of his morning regimen as well.

"I assume you two vagabonds are partners." He sighed painfully, looming over Evie and me like some gigantic canary.

"Yep," I chirped.

"Nope," Evie snapped.

"Wonderful," he said flatly. "As it so happens," he continued, "we—please note I use the empirical we, including *the person currently known by the moniker of Hautelaw Girl,* whatever that means, as part of the group, though I haven't the slightest idea why, since *she* never seems to have time for FFC. Regardless, we have a job to do. And that job, my dears, is to place first at the final show."

"Final *show*?" I said, astonished.

"Had you been on time, you would know that the runway showcase of your final projects is to take place on F-R-I-D-A-Y. For the calendar-challenged among you," he said, glaring at me, "that would be the end of the week."

I opened my mouth to scream *Ohmigod!* but EFKALT held up a warning finger.

"Please do not scream 'ohmigod.' We've been through that already. Now then, I'm *not* going to tell you girls how competitive I am. Nor am I going to tell you that the chance to win a scholarship like this comes along only once in a lifetime and that missing it would mean the ruin of any opportunities you might envision for a possible future in the fashion business. No, I'm *not* going to say that because that would be cruel and unfair. What I *am* going to say is good luck, my darlings . . . you had better win."

With that, he spun on one heel and walked away.

I turned to Evie, hoping to make some inroads toward reconciliation, but she was already shoving her things in her bag.

My face got hot. I searched for something to say. What *could* I say? I had ditched her last night, and she knew it.

"Evie . . ."

When she finally faced me, her glare was tangible. And if looks could kill, I would surely be pushing up daisies.

"Look, I wanted to say something but I couldn't. I mean, I didn't want to hurt your feelings," I offered lamely.

"Oh, you were thinking about *my* feelings? How stupid of me," she retorted sarcastically.

"Evie, Mia knows *everybody*. She has connections. She can help us." I wasn't quite sure what I even meant by that.

"I don't want her help. Or yours! It so happens that Adrianna Heath will be one of the judges on Friday, so I'll have the perfect opportunity to impress her up close. Unlike other *persons*, I don't want anything badly enough that I need to sneak around behind my BFF's back to get it!"

"I wasn't sneaking!"

"Really? What *were* you doing then?"

"I was slipping out for the evening. Is that okay with you? Or do I have to apprise you of every movement I make?"

"That's not fair! I never pry into your business! I just stupidly thought we were in this together!"

"We *are* in this together! I'm doing this for us!"

"You're doing this for you! I would *never* betray your trust!"

"Fine! You want to know why I didn't bring you along? Because Mia asked me not to!"

"Let me guess. I'm not fabulous enough or famous enough to be seen with her and her scrawny friends! Or maybe I'm just not photogenic enough!"

"No, that's not it!" I lied.

"Really? What is it then?"

After a few seconds of dead silence, Evie snorted derisively. "I knew it. So now you just do whatever Mia tells you? Is that it? What happened to BFFs forever?!"

"At least Mia doesn't get into trouble every time she turns around!"

"It's called living, thank you very much! And since when are you so concerned with what other people think?!"

"Maybe I should be!"

Evie's eyes flinched, softening for just a split second. I struggled to say something, anything, to try to get things back on track. But no sooner had I opened my mouth, when my cell phone rang. It was Sheila Hicks.

Unfortunately, that moment of possible reconciliation was gone forever.

"I have to take this," I said, knowing it would be the final nail in my coffin, making me officially *girlena non grata*.

Evie rolled her eyes and stomped off. I pleaded for her to wait. She was at the door already when I said, "Please, just let me explain. I just have to get this one call. . . ."

"Clearly, whoever is calling you is *far* more important than me."

With a heavy heart, I pressed TALK, just as Evie disappeared.

"The publicity is pitch-perfect!" Sheila said. "A candid snapshot of Hautelaw Girl with Mia Meltzer at the hottest club of the moment. I couldn't have arranged it better myself! On second thought, I could have, but what difference does it make? All that matters is that this little item caught the eye of Derek Yates over at Pariah Pictures. He wants to see you chop-chop!"

Unfortunately, it couldn't have come at a worse possible time.

"Sheila," I said weakly, "I can't. Really. I have to be at camp all week. There's a big—"

Sheila's voice instantly went from convivial to firm. "You need to get your priorities straight, young lady. It's time to decide what's more important—a couple of weeks as a camper, or a lifetime as a star?"

She had me there.

chapter twelve

The Deal Breaker

d a t e :   UNKNOWN

To: Devoted Daily Obsession Readers

From: I, Imogene

Re: Sleep deprivation

Chéries,

Did you know that lack of sleep is connected to
obesity?

I mean, if that's not a good enough reason to stay in
bed all day, I don't know what is.

※   ※   ※

Dear All-Knowing and Powerful One,

Never let it be said that it isn't lonely at the top.
Not that I would know the first thing about being
there, because I'm not even close, but I do happen to have
some firsthand experience in what's required to get there.
And what I've discovered is that in spite of one's best efforts

to keep things in balance, there comes a point where life as one knows it comes into conflict with life as one would like to know it. That's where the lonely part comes in.

You'd think by the ripe old age of seventeen I'd have a basic understanding of the workings of the modern world and, for that matter, the cosmos in general. I know, I know, I'm always going on about fate and destiny and all that other stuff because, well, as experience has taught me, there really is something to it. The problem, however, is that when you're in the thick of things, you know, *in the moment*, it's not always easy to remember that there's a bigger plan in motion. Especially when you've worked so hard to make things happen a certain way because there's something else you need to happen so that other things can happen like you want them to. Unfortunately, things are never that simple because, well, people are complicated, which makes it perfectly understandable why relationships can go completely haywire over the littlest thing. Not that Evie and I were at odds over little things. We weren't. For the first time, our friendship was on life support. I knew it was my fault. I was torn between what could be a new future for me and my loyalty to Evie.

Needless to say, it wasn't the best time for Sheila to have arranged yet another meeting. But this one wasn't quite like the others. This one was with Pariah Pictures, one of Hollywood's oldest and most celebrated movie studios, and a meeting there was not something that happened to just anybody, as Sheila was quick to point out. "If Pariah wants to see you, you'd better believe they're serious," she said gravely over the phone. Not that I needed any more pressure, mind you.

As soon as the meeting had ended, I darted out of the Pariah Pictures conference room into the waiting town car that Jools had arranged, faster than the Kate Moss collection flew out of Barneys.

I was in a rush to get back to my hotel room and start writing. Although, for a change, there were mostly only minor comments to the few script pages I had been slowly but steadily writing. In the words of Derek Yates, Pariah's head of production, there was "a somewhat glaring void in my story," which turned out to be a general lack of sex. To what degree I was too nervous to ask, but he suggested I take a crack at juicing up the Paris hotel scenes. (No problem, I lived it!) Of course, they needed it yesterday. And Lord knows how I would ever finish it. (There's that *god-awful* word again — "finish"!)

There was one other thing this time that had me perplexed, though. You see, while we were all sitting around the conference table, Derek's assistant had let it slip that they were deliberating on which of two similar projects to go forward with — mine or someone else's. Who else could be pitching a project like mine? Except for Evie and *moi*, no one else had lived it.

I knew Sheila would have the answer, so when the car exited the parking garage, I punched her number on my iPhone, hoping to get some relief for my low-grade paranoia. Instead I suffered through a boilerplate "out-of-town until Monday" voice message. I didn't bother leaving a message. I mean, at that point I was too freaked out about meeting my deadline to worry about somebody else's project that might or might not be out there, and might or might not be *anything* like mine. The good news was that Evie was going to be out late. She'd sent some cryptic e-mail about having dinner with Marcus, the tech-geek boy, and Fuchsia, an FFC camper Evie had struck up a friendship with. When she announced this, I was able to toss it aside. But thinking of it now, a new feeling lurked beneath the surface. Like I was jealous or something. I mean, I was more than glad that Marcus and Evie liked each other. I was glad to see her IM-ing away with him and scribbling little doodle-y notes to herself about him. But the Fuchsia thing—that had me feeling a smidge . . . uneasy. I never in my worst nightmares dreamt I'd ever be dealing with *BFF ENVY*!

I decided to hunker down and write and just forget about everything else. There was only one problem. When I got back to the hotel and sat down at my computer, I unexpectedly felt a bit flu-ish. I tried piecing an idea together to form a sentence, but I couldn't. My throat became dry and parched. I tried thinking of a word to type. Nothing. Not even my name. I began to shiver, and that's when it hit me: *writer's block*! I've often heard it referred to, but never, *ever* did I imagine it would happen to me.

Five packs of minibar cashews, two macadamia-nut cookies, and four Diet Cokes later, I rolled off the edge of the bed and stood in front of the mirror, gaping at the most hideous raccoon eyes on the planet. I'd been up all night

agonizing. Even a three a.m. vanilla gelato sundae with crushed
pistachios and candied figs (requiring a personal sojourn to
the kitchen, accompanied by shameless pleading) didn't rouse
my literary muse. I mean, I desperately needed to write, but
I didn't *feel* anything, least of all sexy. My stress level rendered
me totally inert.

In addition to my growing paranoia about a competing
movie project, my mind reeled with anxiety about Evie, and
Dustin and Paolo, and Sheila, and finishing what I started,
and now writer's block! Finally, when Toy began to snore, I
burst into tears. It was true. I really couldn't finish *anything*.
I collapsed on the bed and cried until my stomach ached. I
was a complete and utter failure.

I woke with the sun in my eyes. Toy's tongue was on my
face—his not-so-subtle reminder that he needed walking. At
least that would give me a chance to clear my head, to start
thinking up excuses for not finishing my writing. I mean,
who knew? Maybe I'd be hit with some blinding
flash of inspiration.

I looked around for Toy's leash. He had a habit
of running off to some dark corner to chew on it.
I noticed Evie's bed hadn't been slept in. At first
I had a flash of concern, but then I concluded
that she'd do anything at that point to avoid me—she probably crashed with Fuchsia.

"Where's your leash, Toy?"

His response was to spin around in a circle a few times,
then run over to the closet door and yip. Closet, of course! I

was pulling the leash from under a pile of laundry when I happened to glance into my carry-on bag. There, between my Glamontis and my Miu Mius, was a little picture of Paolo and me taken last summer. Paolo was shooting a play for a friend of his and I tagged along. It was one of the best days we had ever spent together. After dinner we went for a long walk in the woods, just talking and, well, you know. I stood there in the dark with my memories and felt a sudden rush of Paolo passion—his hair, his eyes, his lips. I grew flush as my heart rate began to soar. The spell, as they say, was broken! I was ready to write.

The next time I looked at the clock it was ten a.m. I was beyond exhausted, but satisfied at having finished the scenes Pariah had requested.

I hit the send button on my computer, secure in the knowledge that in ten minutes I'd be fast asleep, with nothing on my agenda for the next twenty-four hours.

I was just closing my eyes when the phone rang.

"This is your wake-up call, miss."

At first I was puzzled.

"Is this Miss Imogene?"

"Yes."

"You requested a wake-up call this morning."

"What day is it?"

"It's Saturday, miss."

I sat bolt upright in bed. "Ohmigod, I almost forgot!"

chapter thirteen

The Sting
(As in, Ouch!)

date: MARCH 23

TO-DO LIST:

Check:

Hit the pool for outdoor massage while scanning *Variety*
with story about *moi* in the "Big Deals" section; receive
room service order: caviar, chilled DP rosé; interview
drivers for new Bentley the studio sent over
as a welcome prezzie.

Reality Check:

Give self "insta-mani" (aka bite off fingernails);
chug leftover espresso backwash from nightstand;
drive through killer smog and traffic to get to spa.

T he concierge handed me an itinerary. Hopefully some aspirin would be included for my *Mahabharata*-size migraine.

Saturday: Spa schedule

- **1:00:** Thalaso-therapy. Rejuvenates the stressed-out, sleep-deprived, and overpartied

- **2:00:** Spa box lunch

- **3:00:** Shiroabhyanganasya Friendship Therapy session with spiritual massage therapist

Evie and I had prearranged this date weeks ago—the minute we knew we'd be coming to L.A. But given the state of our relationship, I wondered if she was even here. Better she didn't show up, anyway. I mean, with her around, any kind of relaxation would be impossible.

C learly fate portended this meeting," our spiritual massage therapist, Dyanna, announced solemnly to Evie and me, who lay before her wrapped in white sheets on twin massage tables. Evie was facing the wall. I was facing Evie.

She still wasn't speaking to me, so with no other option than to listen to Dyanna drone on about her touching our joint BFF soul and what her spiritual healing strategy for us was, I zoned out and went into *observer mode*, something we fashion forecasters are quite adept at, if I do say so myself.

Dyanna had fine, birdlike features and a thin frame. She was more diminutive than I'd expect a masseuse to be, though her credentials were anything but. The walls were covered with certificates, accreditations, and commendations from many top schools in the country.

"Now then, I want the two of you to face each other," she said, smoothing lavender oil into her hands before applying them to my shoulders.

Evie didn't budge.

"I can feel your anger," Dyanna said, flinging a solid wall of red hair over her shoulder, "both of you. But to begin the healing process, you must put your egos aside."

She closed her eyes and began waving her hands wildly around us, as if pulling invisible taffy from thin air.

"Your chi is out of balance—it's filled with holes."

Although I couldn't see it, I could feel Evie rolling her eyes. Dyanna was everything Evie found ridiculous about L.A.

"Now," Dyanna whispered, "close your eyes and breathe deeply from within. As you become one with the natural order of things, you will begin to sense each other's energy. Don't resist—let it in. Can you feel it?"

All I could feel was a desire to pull Evie's hair. I nodded my head and peered through one eye to see if Evie was nodding hers. She wasn't, so I squished my eyes shut and tried to focus on my inner truth, but all I could think about was Evie being a selfish jerk.

139

"Now that your energy has merged, I want you both to think back to when you were young, to all the things your friend has done for you over the years."

This was too easy. I mean, when I was seven, Evie deconstructed my entire Barbie wardrobe. And in the fourth grade she decided to open her own beauty school, with me as the first customer—she dyed my hair red with cherry Kool-Aid, then trimmed my eyebrows off. Oh, and when I was eight she talked me into eating fifteen hard-boiled eggs in a row as part of a high-protein diet to help "fill out" my figure, if you know what I mean. Mom had to drive me to the emergency room and have my stomach pumped. To this day I still get bilious anywhere within fifty yards of egg salad. I mean, seriously, the only problem with this exercise was choosing something that hadn't caused me any emotional trauma!

"Okay, ever since we were little Imogene has always been the center of the universe," Evie said out loud.

"What?" I practically shouted.

"Admit it. You're a spotlight junkie."

"I am not," I said, feeling my karmic fury heating up.

"Yeah, you are," she snapped. "Like on my seventh birthday—"

"Ohmigod," I said, "I can't believe you're going to bring that up again."

"You blew out my candles!"

"I was helping!"

"Now Imogene," Dyanna said, "you need to let Evie share. . . ."

"I mean, heaven forbid anyone but *you* should get some attention," Evie interrupted. "It's no wonder you never finish anything—you're too busy stealing the attention from everybody else!"

"Is that what this is about?!" I hollered. "You getting attention?"

"Hey, as long as *you're* around I never have to worry about it! You see to that!"

"Ladies, please," Dyanna said. "Your chi is in tatters!"

"You should see yourself!" cried Evie. "Like last week when you practically *ran* up to the front row at the Tina Lorenz show to be in front of the cameras!" Evie stood up, wrapping her sheet around herself tightly, and did a Paris Hilton. "'Hi, I'm Hautelaw Girl, *love me!*'"

"I was invited, *helloooo*?!"

"So you abandon me?"

"I *knew* you were jealous!"

"I wasn't jealous! I was pissed!"

"Really! I mean, according to you, you're *soooo good* at fashion you don't need me anyway. And I have no doubt I'd be sitting on the sidelines at the FCC finale while *girl wonder* works her magic for all the world to marvel at—especially her idol, Adrianna Heath."

"I can't believe what I just heard."

"You're just not getting it, Evie! This is about the *bigger picture!*"

"What I *get* is that you signed up to be part of a team—remember?!"

We stood there, glaring at each other. For the first time in our lives, Evie and I were out of sync. I knew it, she knew it, and I think it fueled our anger more than just being sick of each other. Don't get me wrong, I was definitely angry. Angry about being late, angry about worrying what Evie was thinking, angry about doing just do what I felt I needed to do. But behind it was something else—something more powerful than my anger. Unwittingly I'd unleashed an earthquake of trouble that, on the Richter scale of one to ten, notched in at eleven. And I realized at that moment that what was fanning the flames of our mutual angst was fear.

I struggled to stay in control, but I could feel my eyes beginning to sting. I soldiered on.

"Why did I expect *you* to understand? Your parents are *skajillionaires*! You never, EVER, *EVER* have to think about the bigger picture! You're made for life! But I'm not! I wasn't born with a silver spoon in my mouth."

"So your plan is to do whatever is necessary to get ahead, is that it?" Evie fumed. "I thought we had a plan for that! I guess you forgot to discuss your *hidden agenda* with me!"

That was the final blow.

"Is that what you think?!" I cried.

"Isn't that what's going on?"

I didn't bother to respond, because at that point it didn't really matter what was said. Our lives had become a trail of good intentions gone haywire. I don't know. Maybe we *had* finally outgrown each other. Maybe I just had to get it through my thick skull that it really *was* time to part company and go our separate ways.

Suddenly I felt so very tired—the kind of tired that makes you want to sleep for a year.

"Maybe we shouldn't be hanging out together anymore," Evie huffed.

"Fine with me," I said courageously. I wasn't about to let Evie know I was near crumbling inside with her last remark.

"Well, that's it then, I guess. Have a good life!"

She had to do that. She had to hit the cry button.

It only happened a few times a year—my hunch was it had something to do with fluctuating hormone levels, but when it hit you, it was like being run over by a bullet train. I'm talking about a song. In particular, the heart-wrenching one that was right this second playing on the car radio. Its haunting lyrics and sad melody were the catalyst for my emotional turmoil. The reality of life without my best friend had finally sunk in, leaving me feeling unhinged in a way I never thought possible. Like I was cut loose in space, adrift, alone in the vastness of some cold, dark, emotional void without a lifeline. I never saw it coming. I was completely decimated, left with nothing but pure, unadulterated misery. And right now, nothing else existed but emotion.

Up until now Evie and I had been inseparable. After all, we were made of the same genetic material (a fluke of nature, since we're not officially related). No longer would I know the greatest feeling in the world—the feeling of being the most important person in someone else's life; the person they ran to when something wonderful or awful happened; the person they'd walk to the ends of the earth for, or climb the highest mountain for; the person they believed in 150 percent.

That was my drive back to Santa Monica.

Now I had to think of other things — like my future. I checked my messages. Sheila, oddly enough, hadn't called back yet. Ashlie, on the other hand, had left seven messages, all of them claiming she had something "very, very important" to tell me. What that was I couldn't imagine, but I decided to meet her anyway. Anything was better than sitting around my empty hotel room, where I'd spent the past week hunched over my computer rewriting my life story.

It's strange, because I'd always imagined life as a writer to be somewhat more charmed—you know, scintillating parties, instant recognition for work well done—but this was just grueling.

Despite my overwhelming gloom, the weather gods had conspired to create an impossibly beautiful sunset. I pulled into Starbucks and found Ashlie sitting at an open-air patio table that jutted out over the ocean. The last remaining rays of sun shone through the horizon line, warming my shoulders, which had suffered from air-conditioned chill all week.

She greeted me with a squinty smile. I hadn't noticed until then how sweet her face was.

"Hey," she said with a hug. "No offense, but you look terrible."

I had thought with a dab of concealer here and there, no one would know I'd spent the past hour sobbing my brains out.

"So what's up?" I said. "Your message sounded urgent."

She hesitated, gazing out across the ocean.

"There's a rumor going around . . ."

Ashlie paused to pour Splenda into her iced tea. "There's another project out there that sounds an awful lot like yours. I thought you should know."

For the moment I remained calm.

"Do you know someone named Brooke? Brooke . . . uh, whatever. I can't think of her last name."

Okay, calm time over. My entire body seized as I struggled to keep from jumping off the edge of the cliff and into the ocean!

"Yup, I know her," I choked.

"Well, first she was hanging around Mia to try to snuggle up to her father. She was so totally desperate to get a movie deal. It was pathetic. Like nobody ever did *that* before. When that failed, she found another way. . . . She got an agent . . . your agent. Mia hooked them up."

The cosmic *gong* went off. I mean, all my fears about someone else having a story out there like mine instantly solidified into a blinding flash of DUH! The other story was Brooke's. Sheila was double-dealing, representing both of us! I felt as though I'd been stabbed in the back. Wait! That's exactly what happened here!

"Why are you telling me this?"

"Friends help friends."

"But you're Mia's best friend."

"I'm getting tired of being another one of Mia's designated drivers."

And there it was, Ashlie's agenda. She wanted to be Mia.

"Of course, Dustin Litchfield . . ." her voice trailed off as she tore open a packet of something. "Biscotti?"

I could feel the blood drain from my face.

"Ashlie," I said as calmly as I could, "what *about* Dustin?"

"Well, Mia told me he was semiattached to your project, and he made friends with you so he could get all the information he could about your boyfriend, Pedro. . . ."

"Paolo."

"Okay, Paolo. But he thinks Brooke's project has a better shot of getting made, so now he's chasing after her."

A second wave of melancholy hit.

"I mean, actors . . ." She rolled her eyes and laughed with an exasperated sigh. "They'll do whatever they have to do to get a juicy part."

I leaned back in my chair as if I'd just had the wind kicked out of me. Again!

"Do you need some water?" the nearby barista said. It sounded as if he were talking through an empty paper towel roll. I zoomed in to focus. His features reminded me of Evie's—black hair, almond eyes, cute turned-up nose. "You don't look so good," he said tentatively, like he was going to call EMS at the first hint of emotional trauma. I couldn't speak. But I could nod my head.

"How could I have been so naive?"

"Welcome to Hollywood."

Before you could say "anger management," I was standing in Sheila's office—eyes burning, gut wrenching, heart racing.

"It's called hedging your bets, darling," Sheila said flatly. "I'm sure you've heard of it."

"But you can't represent her!" I shouted.

"Let's get one thing straight, cookie. No one tells Sheila Hicks who she can or cannot represent," she snapped. "If anyone's going to sell a project like this, it's going to be me. Now sit down and breathe!"

I did as I was told. Sheila slid from behind her desk and stood in front of me, hands on hips.

"It's time you grew up, little girl. This isn't some little party game with your friends. This is hardball, and people get hurt! That's how it is!" She leaned back on her desk and folded her arms. "Usually I don't bother explaining my actions because frankly, it's nobody's business why I do the things I do as long as I get results—which I do. If they don't like it, they can go crying to some other agent who gives a damn. But since I genuinely like you, I'm going to fill you in. *Just this once!*"

I mumbled a thank-you.

"First of all, Brooke came to me long before I ever spoke to you. And yes, your stories are similar."

I opened my mouth, but she stopped me.

"Don't ask, because I won't tell you. No more than I would tell her about your project. What I will say is that I think yours is better. Not that Brooke's isn't good, it's very good—she has talent, but yours has a certain vitality to it . . . an energy. And Pariah agrees."

"You heard from them?" I ventured.

"Derek called me last night. He wants to move forward with it right away. I was about to call you when you burst in here."

I would have apologized if I hadn't been so busy peeling myself off the ceiling.

"They've already assigned an executive producer and writer to move the project forward," she added.

"But I thought I was going to write it."

"Please, I just said you were a good writer. You did a great job with the changes. For what it's worth, it helped sell the project—Derek *loved* whatever it was you gave him. There's only one last change they want to make to the story. I told him I'd discuss it with you, but I didn't think it would be a problem."

My heart was pounding so hard I could barely get the words out of my mouth.

"If I agree to the change, I'll have a deal?"

"And everything that comes with it," Sheila said, sitting down at her desk. "They want to franchise the whole thing. That means TV, Internet, books, games, you name it . . .

you'll be a *very wealthy* young lady. Not to mention an international icon."

"What's the change?"

"It's the sidekick issue. They think the Evie character takes the spotlight away from Hautelaw Girl—it should just be about her and her dog. In other words, lose the BFF."

Lions, and Tigers, and Agents, Oh My (Gawd)!!

date: MARCH 23

To: Tout le monde

From: Imogene

Re: In reality, here's what California, aka the land
of fruits and nuts, is full of: earthquakes, smog,
traffic jams, spirit guides, chakra tuners, tantric
healers, aura readers, massage therapists, air-kissers,
plastic surgery hogs, and fakes. Need I remind
you of the eighteenth rule of style?
"Fake is never in fashion!"

t's funny how life can change in a heartbeat. One day everything is going along the way it always does—the sun comes up, birds twitter, fish swim, and the big old earth keeps spinning around, and the next day, *voilà*, out-and-out ruination! Oh well, I've always wanted to join the Peace Corps.

It's hard to imagine, but just two weeks ago Evie and I were best friends forever and Caprice was a wildly single supermodel. And then, without the slightest warning, *POOF!* Everything that I thought would last forever was no more. As for Sheila, well, needless to say, she was not exactly delighted when I told her I needed a little time to think about removing Evie from the story (though it was a smidge tempting, given the state of our relationship). She warned me that if I stalled, Pariah Pictures would option Brooke's story instead of mine and I'd be left with nothing. Fortunately, I was spared the old cliché, "And you'll never work in this town again," but then it didn't need to be said—it was abundantly clear.

We parted company. I left telling her I'd call in the morning, after I'd had a chance to get used to the idea of cutting Evie out of the story. But I never did—call her, I mean. Instead I frittered away the day at the beach, lost in a haze of indecision. I brought Toy—whose only expectations of me were food and the occasional fit of unbridled affection—and went for a long walk along the beach, soaking up sun and ignoring several thousand calls from Jools.

Back in my room, a manila envelope from SHE marked EXTREMELY URGENT was waiting for me. It was the contract from Pariah Pictures for the rights to my story—complete with ominous legalese and a Day-Glo red Post-it stuck in the center with the words I WANT THIS BY FIVE P.M.! printed in big, black Sheila letters. It was an eerie feeling, standing there in a bathing suit, holding my entire future in my hands. I mean, all I had to do was sign on the dotted line and a life of untold riches, fame, and everything else a girl such as I could ever wish for would be mine. Well, almost.

When Caprice called, it was close to three o'clock. I was still sitting on the bed, staring at the document. I hadn't read it. She asked if I would meet her for one last "single girls" shopping spree at Barneys—you know, shoes, lingerie, honeymoon outfit, more shoes. Normally this was something that went under the heading of "thrill ride," but with the recent plague of personal pandemonium, it turned out to be more of a funeral march. As desperate as I was to get some sound advice about the disaster I refer to as "my life," it wasn't to be. Caprice was in launch mode, as in T-minus 127 hours until "till death do you part" and counting; while I, wounded, pathetic, and BFF-less, was obliged to suppress

any visible signs of my tormented soul. I mean, it was clear there was a lot more on Caprice's mind than ready-to-wear.

After a few hours of shopping, our mission was accomplished. As we were passing through children's apparel on our way out, we stopped for a second to laugh at some adorable Icky Baby bibs when it happened—Caprice broke down, right there in the middle of Barneys. I steered all 34-24-36 of her into a nearby dressing room and plied her with tissues.

I'm sorry," she cried, sitting down. "When I saw those bibs I just couldn't help myself."

"Ohmigod! You're not . . ."

"WHAT?! NO! It's just that they remind me of when I was little," she hiccupped. "Life was so uncomplicated then."

A fresh wave of boo-hoos and nose blows washed her thought away. Which left nothing for me to do but hold the tissues and wait for her to calm down. To tell the truth, the whole thing was beginning to make me a little weepy too— not that I needed any help in that department.

Eventually Caprice came up for air. "It's not that I don't love Eddie," she sobbed. "I'm crazy about him."

"He wants you to quit your career?" I ventured.

"Never! He loves what I do. It gives him something to brag about to his friends."

"I don't get it."

Caprice turned to me and smiled sadly, her eyes red, mascara smeared.

"When I was a girl in Puerto Rico," she began, "I used to sit in my room every day and look at magazines for hours. The walls were covered with pictures I'd cut out—even on the ceiling." She laughed. "I *knew* someday I would be a model, or an actress, or both. It drove my mother crazy because when all my friends were outside playing, I was practicing expressions in front of the mirror, or reading Stanislavski, or Naomi Campbell's biography, or anything that would help me reach my goal. For my twelfth birthday

I made my father build a runway out of old plywood in our backyard so I could practice my walk. All the other girls made fun of me, but I didn't care. I knew what I was doing. One afternoon I wrote it all down—a plan. What I wanted to be and how to get there. I rubbed red lipstick on my hand as a blood oath and *swore* to stick to it no matter what. I always keep it with me no matter where I go."

Her story set off an alarm somewhere deep inside me, but for some reason I couldn't quite put my finger on what it was. Maybe I was too tired. Or maybe I just didn't want to hear it. Whatever it was, it made me very uncomfortable.

"So now you're a famous model," I said, pointing out the obvious. "Soon to be an actress, and—"

"And the other day I took out my piece of paper and read it again. Marriage is *not* part of the plan! Not yet, anyway."

"You're off course."

"This is why we're friends, Imogene!" Caprice dabbed her eyes. "You understand what it means to stick to your guns. You want to be a great fashion diva and you *will be*, because you know exactly what it is you want. You're always on course!"

I almost herniated myself trying not to cringe. Obviously she'd been too busy with her in-laws to keep up with the gossip columns; otherwise she'd know I was so far off course no GPS in the world could find me—even I couldn't find me, and I was sitting right there. Caprice took my hands in hers and looked at me pleadingly.

"I'm so worried about my family," she sobbed. "They want this so much. And after all the work Eduard's family has done to make this happen . . . I just don't know what to do!"

The hypocrite in me went to work.

"Be true to yourself, Caprice. Just because other people have plans for you doesn't mean you have to go through with them. The marriage will wait. And if it doesn't, well then, it wasn't meant to be in the first place."

Okay, I know what you're thinking. And frankly, if I were you I'd be shaking my head too. But you know what? It's easy to straighten out other people's lives, because you're not in the thick of things—emotionally, I mean. Not to mention, you don't have to face the consequences of your *own advice*—in this case, good advice, thank you very much. Unfortunately, the better Caprice felt, the gloomier I felt. To make matters worse, on the way out she asked how Fashion Camp with Evie was going. I'd lied enough for one evening, so I mumbled "Grape," hoping she'd think I said "Great."

"Did you say *grape*?" she asked.

"Why would I say grape?" I chuckled nervously.

I managed to escape further embarrassment when I realized I'd left a bag in the dressing room and rushed back inside to get it.

By the time I was back outside, Caprice had strolled to the end of the block. It was getting late and traffic had thinned out for the day, leaving the street strangely empty. An approaching storm blotted out the last of the sunset, filling the sky with an ominous blanket of black and purple clouds. Along Wilshire the giant palms began to creak and sway in a sudden burst of chilly air. To be honest, the whole thing was a tad eerie. A flash of lightning ripped across the sky. I shut my eyes tightly as everything that had happened over the past week came flooding back to me. I mean, how could I have been so easily swayed by these people, just going along with them like an idiot without question. What they wanted wasn't *my* story, but some Frankenstein version, which had nothing to do with me or my life or my truth at all. Unless I actually stole the Persimmon Diamond and nobody told me about it. And Evie. How could I have given up on her so easily? I mean, she was a part of that truth. Part of what defined me as a person. In her own crazy way she's always kept me on course, moving toward a finite point that was my destiny. And it was not, I repeat *not*, to be rewritten for a bunch of people who neither knew me, cared about me, or most important, believed in me. Not like Evie. My destiny was only to be written by me, one day at a time, and maybe, if I was lucky, with a little help from my BFF. I thought of Evie, and all her talent. And me, wrapped up in all my hopes and dreams. And it hit me: We'll never be able to realize our dreams without each other.

The first droplets of rain began to fall.

I raced back to the hotel, but Evie was nowhere to be found. Her cell wasn't picking up either—not even a message. In a panic I hit the front desk, thinking she might be winging her way back to Greenwich. She was still checked in.

I called Sheila and left a brief message. I would not be signing the contract, but I thanked her for her time and effort. Then I walked into the closet, closed the door, and cried for a very, very long time.

By eleven the storm had turned into a deluge, complete with thunder and lightning. I flopped on my bed, staring at a blank TV screen, hoping it might transmit some type of subconscious message as to Evie's whereabouts. Even Toy, who was busy chewing on the corner of the pillowcase, looked confused. Then it occurred to me—with the final show being only four days away, Evie had to be *somewhere*, working on the project.

After a few well-placed calls, I found myself barreling down the coast toward Marina del Rey in the driving rain.

Fuchsia met me at the door.

"I'm guessing the spa wasn't really helpful," Fuchsia said ruefully.

"Does Evie know I'm here?"

"You said, 'Don't say anything,' so I didn't."

Fuchsia led me up a palatial staircase, down a hallway wide enough for two-lane traffic, and into a room that had been commandeered for a design studio, complete with dress forms, a trimming table, and a sewing machine. Fabric, drawings, scissors, tapes, and other paraphernalia were scattered everywhere, and the floor was littered with scraps of material. The dress forms were blank. Evie lay prostrate on the sofa. She didn't bother to look up. Fuchsia quickly excused herself on the pretense of making tea or something, and left the two of us alone.

"Evie," I said carefully.

"Made your deal, did you? When's the press conference?"

"Actually, there is no deal."

Evie slowly turned her head and looked directly me. Her eyes were bright, almost feverish.

"Do you want the short story, or the long?"

"Whichever way you want," Evie replied quietly.

"I couldn't finish it, so they dumped me."

"I don't understand."

"You know me." I chuckled. "I'm a great starter, but not a great finisher."

Evie stood up slowly. Her shoulders were sloped and she had dark circles under her eyes. It was obvious she hadn't done much sleeping either.

"You don't give yourself enough credit," she stammered. "And what about your story? You worked so hard on it."

"I'll just have to *live* my story. Anyway, I didn't come here to talk about that. I came to apologize."

She started to say something, but I put my hand up to stop her. I wanted to tell her exactly how I felt while I still had it in me. I blinked and began to see Evie as a little girl again. The one I used to play dress-up in my room with, the one I snuck up to the roof of Aunt Tamara's New York apartment at the Sherry Netherland with during Christmas to watch the snowfall over Fifth Avenue, the one I helped with the fashion show for our third-grade class, when we decided that nude was the new black. (My parents never recovered from that one—nor did anyone else's, for that matter.)

It was crystal clear that Evie was one of those rare individuals who could make so much more out of life than what it handed her, that she had the gift of transforming the ordinary into the extraordinary, and do it with all the unbounded energy, and humor, and goodwill she had in her. And even though things hadn't always worked out for the best, they had *never, ever* been boring. Not for a second.

I vowed never to tell Evie the nasty details about why my deal fell through. I suppose I had always known somewhere deep down in my soul that even if I'd signed that contract, and got all the money, and all the fame, and all the other stuff that came with it, I would have spent my days with people like Mia and Dustin and Sheila, whose only interest in me was what they could get out of it for themselves. And I guess that's what finally changed my mind. I mean in the end, even if Evie and I never achieved true fashion greatness (perish the thought), at least we'd have had an absolute blast trying.

"I'm so sorry, Evie," I said, choking back tears. "I'm sorry because I was a crummy friend and put myself before everything else that really matters in a friendship. And most of all, I'm sorry because I hurt your feelings."

Evie burst into tears and ran to me with a huge hug.

"No, I'm sorry!" she cried. "It was my fault for being jealous of you. I should have been supportive, but I wasn't. I was only thinking of myself, of how I could impress Adrianna Heath."

After hugs and more "I'm sorry"s, I broke out an emergency box of petit fours from my bag.

At this Evie perked up. "You're not just doing that to make me feel better, are you, girlena?"

We both laughed and swore never to go through this ever again, no matter what.

Fuchsia came back with tea, and the conversation turned to the show—more important, how the assignment was going. Apparently, they'd both been struggling since Friday, without much success.

"I have a lot of good ideas, girlena," Evie heaved. "But we need something really spectacular to *win*. Something that will totally blow everyone away."

"What's needed is a concept," I said.

"Exactly," Evie agreed. "And a way to *project* that to the audience in a way they've never seen before."

A bolt of pure inspiration hit. I stood up and shouted, "Evie, you just said it!"

"What?"

Every nerve in my body tingled and my heart pounded a million beats a second.

"Project the image!" I said slowly. "Get it?!"

I paused, struggling to put my thoughts together.

"Remember the frog prince, Evie? You know, the one from Spellman's office . . . the virtual rain forest?"

"Yeah . . ."

"Marcus is a hologram expert, right?" I said.

Evie's eyes grew as wide as saucers. She could see exactly what I could see, just like always.

chapter Fifteen

The Kid Stays in the Picture

date: MARCH 26

mood: FASHION ADDICTION

Fashion is like a magnet.
Once you get a taste of it, you're in for good.
You can try to run away from it,
to say you're going to be a teacher, or a lawyer, or a doctor,
but at the end of the day,
it's always there to pull you right back in.

* * *

pinned a vintage moonstone-and-ruby brooch onto my lapel, smooched on a dab of Lancôme Pout-à-Porter lip gloss (never let it be said that I don't do my best to further chic in the world), and climbed into the backseat of the SUV (aka FFC transport). Evie and I were back on track, and I hadn't felt this great in ages.

Inside, the atmosphere was electric. Everyone was texting, blogging, diarizing, and gossiping about the final Fashion Fantasy Camp showdown. Someone flipped on the satellite TV:

"Today, more than one hundred lucky fashion fans will be among the celebrity guests for the first-ever Fashion Fantasy Camp fashion show. Hi, everyone, I'm Missy Farthington, and I'm standing in front of the celebrated Kodak Theatre in Hollywood, California, the scene of this very special event. Fashion students from all over the country have been working day and night to come up with fabulous designs that will be judged by some of fashion's ranking nobility. And models? Let's just say that if Naomi can't make these clothes look good, well . . . Wait! I think I see Jock Lord stepping out of a limo. . . . Let's see if we can grab him before he goes inside. Mr. Lord! Jock? Hello . . . ?"

I, for one, couldn't have been more relieved. Not that I wasn't nervous about the show or anything, because I was perfectly bonkers, but now that I was back on track with my plan to dominate the fashion galaxy (BFF at my side), there wasn't anything that could possibly throw me, or so I thought.

Of course, there had been a lot of catching-up to do, which meant the rest of the week was completely and utterly crazed. And with our idea in place, there were a gazillion details to be worked out. Evie and I had spent much of the time shuttling between our hotel room, the conference room at FFC, the theatre, and Marcus's workshop.

Marcus had turned out to be brilliant. Not to mention completely (officially) smitten with Evie (and vice versa). His workshop was in the garage of an old forties bungalow that his grandfather, an inventor (the man who patented the electric lemon zester, among other things), had left him, and, as luck would have it, right around the corner from Fred Segal. Yay!

We had worked furiously, inputting designs, writing programs, smooching (Evie and Marcus only), and testing tracking software. I took it from there, styling the collection with finishing touches like shoes, bags, and a touch of jewelry. The time frame was killer. It was do or die.

We were about to wrap things up when Evie crept into the room holding a copy of *Daily Variety*. I could tell by her expression that there was something she wanted me to see, but didn't quite know how to go about it.

"Don't worry, sweetie," I said reassuringly, "I've been expecting it."

But it wasn't what I'd expected. There, in big, black letters, boldly proclaiming for all the world to see, were the words:

HICKS NIX PITS PIX

Hollywood. March 26.

Legendary agency bigwig Sheila Hicks has thrown over two "life in the fashion lane" projects from burgeoning East Coast fashionistas, Hautelaw Girl and Brooke B., for West Coaster Mia Meltzer, daughter of producer Milos Meltzer. The screenplay for Ms. Meltzer's story about a young fashionista who struggles to make it in the movie biz is currently being penned. Attached to play the male lead is up-and-comer Dustin Litchfield. According to sources, Meltzer may also make her acting debut in the movie, provided she stays out of trouble. Ms. Meltzer was released under her own recognizance by police yesterday and is confined to her home pending sentencing for a second DUI arrest Monday night. Hicks doesn't anticipate any difficulties at the arraignment, and all lights remain green for the upcoming production. Meltzer Senior's company, Megalomania Entertainment, will exec produce, along with Pariah Pictures' Derek Yates.

"I'm so sorry, girlena," Evie said softly.

She had mistaken the sudden flush and bleary-eyed look of rage on my face for sadness. I mean, it was enough that I had abandoned the project—that was a choice I made, and I could live with it—but to discover that Mia had played me the whole time was just too much. All that business about hanging out with her, and going to clubs, and her being *so interested* in me was just so she could pick my brain, to find out what I was up to! *And I helped her!* I honestly thought I was going to explode.

Evie gazed on sympathetically, unsure what to say.

My cell phone rang. I decided to answer it rather than crush it with my bare hand.

"Yessss," I hissed.

"Don't get excited, this isn't a social call."

My spine stiffened. "Brooke?" I said, completely stunned.

"Have you seen the trades yet?"

"The trades?"

"Duh! As in, *Variety*?"

"You mean Mia's deal?"

"That little double-dealing traitor!" she fumed. I could just see her narrowing her tarantula eyes. "No doubt she combined *our* stories to make hers!"

"But I thought . . ."

"Funny, isn't it? Sheila's been working with me since February. I thought I'd cornered the market until you showed up—there's just no accounting for taste. I mean, Hautelaw Girl," she snorted. "How completely stupid."

"I can't believe Sheila would—"

"Don't blame Sheila. She does what she does. It's business. But Mia's just a no-talent party girl. I should have known better than to tell her anything!"

"So you called to vent."

"Hardly. I called to gloat. *And* to set the record straight."

"I still don't get it."

"You really are thick. Do you honestly think I didn't figure out Mia was trying to play me . . . with Dustin and her daddy in Sheila's office? Sheila didn't dump me, I pulled my project out of there days ago." Brook chuckled. "I'm way too good for this town."

"Does that mean you won't be at the final FFC show?"

"Of course I will. But funny thing about that. I was on my way to dinner last night and thought I'd stick my head in the theater for a second — just to get the lay of the land, you know? And to my surprise, your little friend Evie and her smooch buddy were doing some kind of test. It didn't really amount to much, but if it's any indication of what's in store for the show, well . . . it's going to be . . . awesome."

I had to stop and catch my breath. I mean, I always knew I'd live to grow old, and I was pretty sure I'd see people land on Mars, but never in my wildest dreams did I think I'd live to hear anything remotely like *that* from Brooke.

"Excuse me, was that a compliment I just heard?"

"No. And don't you ever, *ever* tell anybody we spoke today! I have a reputation to protect."

"Absolutely not," I swore.

"Remember, after this it's back to business as usual. I hate you, and you . . . well, you do whatever it is that someone like you does."

There was a resounding *click*, and that was that—phone call over.

"Who was that?" Evie asked.

"An old frenemy," I replied.

So that was then and this was, well, show day. The greenroom (which was actually a rather obscure shade of vermilion) was a madhouse, packed with frantic fashion students, models, hair and makeup artists, and production crew, all of whom were working on last-minute details. And FYI, if that wasn't enough pressure, there were more than a thousand people packed in the theater who'd be watching it all.

The show had already started. I managed to find a quiet spot behind one of the monitors to watch.

I was completely mesmerized by the glittering cast of judges, when a rose appeared before my eyes. Don't worry, there was a hand attached. I twirled around and there stood Dustin.

"What are *you* doing here?" I snapped.

"I don't blame you for being upset," he said.

"You haven't answered my question."

"I'm here to explain. I don't expect you to understand, but I wanted to tell you anyway."

He took a step forward. "I wanted

you to know just how hard it is for an actor to get ahead in this business."

I thought he would say more. Instead he searched my eyes for a reaction.

"That's very helpful information. Now if you don't mind, I'm on camera in a few minutes."

"That's my line," he joked.

"No. Your line is, 'Would it be crude of me to pick your brain about Paolo?'"

"Touché. It was a lousy thing to do."

"That's putting it mildly."

I turned to leave, but he placed a hand on my shoulder. "Wait. Please. Just hear me out."

I eyed him warily. The thing about actors is you're never really sure if they are being themselves or someone else. But given all the lapses in judgment I myself have had recently, I was in a forgiving mood.

"I'm listening."

"This business pays well . . . okay, very well. That's part of it," he said, contemplatively. "You know—the 'golden handcuffs' thing. I've been on the verge of stardom for a long time now . . . people promising the big part but never delivering, movie deals gone bad, waiting for the call that puts you over the top and keeps you there . . . forever."

He paused briefly, watching my eyes for a flicker of understanding.

"Anyway, I've been trying to get in front of Mia's dad for ages. Even Sheila, with all her pull, couldn't do it—he's that big. When Mia approached me about her movie . . ."

"Wait a minute, Sheila didn't arrange it?"

"Not at all. Milos went to Sheila about the deal because his daughter needed an agent. And she's the best. I should have told you, I know."

"Did you know that night on the beach?"

"Absolutely not. Mia called me the next day."

Okay, so maybe he was telling the truth. Maybe not. Either way, there was nothing to do about it. I mean, I really did like him. There was just something deep down, something genuine that in another lifetime might have become very real.

I glanced across the room at Evie, buzzing around from model to model, taking care of all the little details, as happy as I'd ever seen her. *This* was my life. *This* was what I wanted.

"I still haven't heard the *S*-word," I said playfully.

He proffered the rose. "You're right, I'm sorry." He smiled back. "I know I made a mistake—a big one. But I won't make it again. Promise."

He stepped closer. His fire opal eyes shimmered.

"If you'd only stay in L.A. a little while longer . . ."

"I can't," I said half sad, half glad.

He smiled an understanding smile, and gently put his hand on my cheek and whispered, "Another time, another place."

QUIIIIIIET!" Peter, the floor director, shouted from the center of the room. A tense hush fell over the crowd.

"Thank you. All right, here's how it's going to work, people. Each group will come out *on my cue*. You'll have exactly three minutes to talk about your ideas, and then your models will do their thing. Got it?! Now get hot, everybody! Remember, you're all going out there as Fashion Fantasy Campers, but only some of you will come back as stars!" He stopped to chat into his headset for a moment, glanced at his clipboard, then checked his watch. "Okay, first group, House of Balenciaga, you're on in six minutes! Follow me!"

While Balenciaga nervously scurried behind him, models in tow, everyone crowded around the monitors to watch. It was fun, like a game show—ten minutes on and off the catwalk, and everyone applauded. I half expected the judges to hold up a scorecard.

In what seemed like no time, House of Balenciaga was back in.

"Okay, House of Dior!" Peter hollered. "Let's go! You're up next."

The tension was mounting. All I could do was inwardly scream *OMG, OMG, OMG!!* In the midst of my fifty-third *OMG*, Brooke, out of nowhere, grabbed me by the elbow.

"Good luck," she whispered. Before I could react, a sudden burst of chatter filled the room as the House of Dior had already returned and everyone rushed over to compare notes.

"House of Chanel!" Peter announced. "You're up next!"

Evie rushed to my side. "That's us!"

"Remember, fashion is only a spectator sport if you're *not*

in the game." Brooke sighed. "And you're here not only to play, but to win."

I swear I detected a proud tear as she spun on her heels and vanished into the crowd. Of course, Evie and I both almost fainted.

Peter was waiting with a phalanx of PAs to escort us through the backstage corridors populated by set scenery and props. As we neared the stage, echoes from the audience grew louder with laughter and applause, but my heart was beating so loudly I could barely hear myself think.

After what seemed like an eternity, Peter stopped at the edge of the stage and held his hand up. The models were quickly shuttled into place while Evie and I nervously waited behind a side curtain just slightly taller than the Great Wall of China. It blocked our view of the audience, but we had a full view of the long white runway. Oh yes, and Cory, the emcee. (Natch!) She was *only* standing about ten feet away, introducing *us* to the audience! I have a new appreciation for how pro football players must feel when they get ready to run out onto the field for a game—the megarush of adrenaline as the crowd roars, the nervous excitement of not knowing what's going to happen next.

Evie took my hand and gave it a familiar squeeze, and off we went toward the stage.

"Here we go, girlfriend!" she shouted.

The lights dimmed, the house music began to thump, and the first supermodel strutted out onto the runway, clad in nothing more than a green body suit, studded with little reflective dots. Audience reaction was exactly as expected. A few chuckles here, hushed comments there. But when the holographic projectors kicked in and like magic, beamed a magnificent reinterpretation of Anita Ekberg's evening dress from *La Dolce Vita* onto the model, the audience literally gasped. I mean, it was perfect! She walked to the end of the runway, shifted her hips, pouted, and slinked back with the projected holographic dress moving on her body as if it were the real thing. For the next ten minutes, model after model walked out on the runway, swathed in three-dimensional illusions of Evie's stunning collection, until the last model vanished into the darkness of the rear curtains.

The music stopped, the lights didn't come up, and the audience leaped to their feet with a roar of applause, cheering and shouting, "Encore!" Even the judges stood and clapped as Evie dragged me and a reluctant and mortified Marcus on the stage for a well-deserved bow. The Houses and their models were then brought back onstage for the judges' final verdict—which was tense, *to say the least*! I mean, with House of Dior's spin on Film Noir gowns (black-and-white only, natch) the impeccable craftsmanship from the House of Balenciaga with their neo–Doctor Zhivago collection, and our techo-Italian cinema redux, the jury's decision wouldn't be easy. It had all the makings of a classic cliffhanger.

chapter ſixteen

Terms of Endearment

date: MAY 15

To: Imogene

Fr: Paolo

Mi Amore,

Running to the airport to pick up my parents. Mom can't wait to meet you. Don't forget, curtain time is 7 p.m. Sorry I couldn't make the "wedding."

xo

P

*   *   *

t's true what they say: There really *is* nothing more beautiful than a bride on her wedding day. Personally, I happen to be a big blubberer when it comes to knot tying, so I always bring an extra box of tissues just for the occasion—but enough about me. This was Caprice's moment, and a more beautiful bride there never was.

She was the picture of grace and poise as she stepped down the aisle—her veil sparkling with a thousand hand-embroidered diamonds from the esoteric ateliers of Paris; her dress, a symphony of cascading camellia-embroidered elegance; her hair, a poem of gently falling curls; and her smile, well . . . it was more of a grin, actually.

"Cut! Cut! Hold it!"

The director stepped from behind the camera and strode toward Caprice.

"Caprice, dearest," he cooed. "You're supposed to be a blushing bride, not a grinning one. You look like you just won the trifecta!"

"Sorry." She giggled madly. "I thought I was supposed to be happy."

"Nobody's *that* happy on their wedding day, believe me. Now please . . . Caprice, honey. Tone it down."

I took another tissue from the box and blew my nose. It's funny how people from Los Angeles get so worked up over a little production. The only thing I can figure is it has something to do with the latitude, or the sun, or both, because it certainly has nothing to do with the natives. I mean, of all the people I met there, only a handful had actually been born on California soil. Whatever it is, it certainly makes them crazy about all things cinema.

But that has nothing to do with today because here we were back in good old New York, shooting on a stage, with cameras, and actors, and producers, and effects, and catering, and everything else that goes with it—just like L.A. The only difference is, when I'm done here I can dine at Serendipity or swoon over the treasures at MOMA, or stroll down Fifth Avenue. And hey, if I need a beach, well, there's always the Hamptons.

Caprice, if you haven't already guessed, is still single. And the good news is, it's all good news. I mean, she and Eddie are still together and have promised their families that they will, most definitely, get married one of these days. Not that the parents are exactly thrilled, mind you, but it's better than no wedding at all. She did land a small part in a movie, but that doesn't start shooting for another week, so she's doing what most actors do when they're not acting—commercials!

"Take twenty-seven!" the assistant director shouted, snapping the clapboard.

"And . . . action." The director sighed, rising above the set atop his crane following Caprice: demure, blushing, with just a shadow of a smile on her beautiful lips, as she walked flawlessly down the aisle.

At the altar she turned. White rose petals began falling like a gentle snow, shrouding the ground poetically. Bridesmaids rushed forward, anxious to catch the bouquet.

Caprice aimed the bouquet, and something caught my eye. Her wrist snapped and the flowers soared through the rarified atmosphere in a long, high arc. There was a brief flicker as it passed through the studio lights, creating the illusion of slow motion as it tumbled gently downward, falling,

falling, falling. Past the intended bridesmaids, and right toward me! Suddenly, I was caught up in the action. I was determined that nothing would prevent me from catching the bouquet. When I did, something cold jangled in my palm. Caprice's charm bracelet had come loose. Dangling from one of its links was a single golden charm, encrusted with the rarest of fire opals. It was beyond breathtaking. When I finally managed to pry my eyes away from its beauty, I caught sight of Caprice. She was already looking at me, the corners of her mouth turned up into the most mischievous smile. I waved the bracelet above my head to let her know she'd lost it.

She shook her head. "It's for you," she mouthed. "From Dustin."

I turned back to the charm, which had been warming in my hands. When I flipped it over, I noticed it had been beautifully engraved with just two words: GOLDEN HANDCUFFS.

Stardust Memories

date: LATE FALL

mood: TWINKLY, SHIMMERY, SHINY

❋　❋　❋

Other than shopping, there was only one thing that could have brought us into NYC on a frosty December afternoon, and that was the burning of Atlanta.

Evie had managed to score a couple of screening passes to the remake of *GWTW* from Marcus. In fact, it was Marcus who had spotted us in one of the effects shots he worked on, and he insisted we go.

In the long run, the media spin about the fire had been rather brilliant. Spellman, known for his digital extravaganzas, claimed to have returned to his filmmaking roots by using practical effects, as he was quoted, "out of respect for the traditions of the industry and as a tribute to this great and historic film." It looked good in the trades, anyway.

And speaking of L.A., in case you're wondering what happened with the Fashion Fantasy Camp final show — well, after three long and arduous votes, the jury had remained deadlocked — which meant we were *all* winners. Not exactly the glorious victory Evie had hoped for, but at least she had her day in the sun with Adrianna Heath. After the show, Evie went to see her, intent on begging for a summer internship. But it turned out Evie didn't have to beg. Adrianna would be doing the costumes for an upcoming Broadway musical and promised Evie a job if she would be interested. (Duh!)

Though Brooke and I had a brief moment of friendship, it didn't amount to much. She went right back to hating me as soon as I returned home. Though, I must admit, it was nice while it lasted.

As for Mia and Ashlie, well, they've been gracing the gossip columns for a while now. Mia had another run-in with her friend, "Crystal," and wound up cooling her Jimmy Choo heels in rehab for three months, just long enough for her movie deal to tank and Ashlie Mortimer to climb into her inebriated size sevens.

Dustin's attachment to Mia's project, needless to say, went the way of Mia's movie deal. Though, happily, Dustin did not. I mean, when you think of it, the odds of getting a movie made are even worse than the likelihood of a single atom splitting in a Large Hadron Collider — a one in fifty million chance of a particle collision so powerful that it could destroy our entire solar system. Fortunately, there's never a shortage of movie deals in Hollywood. And I'm happy to report that Dustin had already been signed to two potential blockbusters.

For a while there we were e-mailing several times a week, uneasily agreeing that together we were better as friends. But as the time between us grew, our correspondence has become less and less. Besides, hanging with my BFF Evie, *mi amore* Paolo, and my alter ego Toy keeps me too busy for a Hollywood pen pal.

One good thing—Caprice emerged as one of four finalists for the role of Honey Dripper, a rogue spy romanced by the shaken, but not stirred, James Bond. The script is so hush-hush that when asked, Pariah Pictures reps declined to comment. As has Caprice. She's not the kind who lets stardom go to her head—like yours truly, for instance.

And speaking of me, well, for the first time in my life I actually finished something I started. Granted, there were a few hairpin turns and a near-BFF catastrophe along the way, but the way I look at it, having had my own personal star rise and fall over the course of spring break, the meaning of that childhood event has finally become clear. I mean, when you really think about it, the universe is made up of all different kinds of stars: red dwarfs, blue giants, binary stars, and polestars. There are stars that rise quickly and burn out in a flash—those are shooting stars like Mia and Ashlie. And there are stars that burn practically forever, the ones that are forged from heat and pressure over a lifetime. Those are the stars that burn the steadiest, the ones that provide light and purpose to the planets that surround them, that bring strength to all that shares in their warmth. That's the kind of star I hope to be. With or *without* Hollywood! Besides, what's the hurry? At seventeen, I've got the rest of my life ahead of me. Plenty of time for twinkle, shimmer, and shine. And speaking of twinkle, Evie tells me I can rest assured that my *la dolce vita* has returned, one hundred percent—and then some. As I sat there in the dark movie theater, thinking about the most significant people in my short and happy life, I realized how lucky I was to have them, with all their wonderful madness, as a part of my own personal galaxy. I saw everything so very clearly then, a picture of how great (with the exception of the odd asteroid falling to earth) my life was.

"Girlena, pay attention!" Evie whispered, lisping on a Gummy Bear. "This is it!"

I snuggled deeper into my chair and smiled contentedly at the affirmation: *Good friends are like stars. You don't always see them, but you know they are always there.*

When the picture was over, we wandered out of the movie lobby into the chilly night air. The hustle and bustle of NYC streets swarmed and swayed with cheerful pedestrians as they crisscrossed the avenues, bound for wherever their destiny sent them.

While Evie hailed a cab, I gazed up at the flickering silver stars, so close I felt as though I could reach up and touch them. I smiled. Just to the right of Orion was an old, and very dear friend, come back at last. As Evie stepped into the cab, a feeling of contentment washed over me, and I was transported to another place—a place filled with happiness. I knew then that whatever fate had in store for me I'd be all right. Better than all right.

I threw my bag into the cab, and just before I closed the door, I gave my star one last glance, and for a brief moment, I could have sworn that somewhere far, far away, a coyote howled.

FADE TO PINK
(After all, it's my movie!)

The adorable, delicious—
and trés stylish—adventures of
Imogene are delighting readers
around the globe.
Don't miss these darling favorites!

By Lisa Barham

From Simon Pulse
Published by Simon & Schuster

What's life without a little . . .

DRAMA!

★ A new series by Paul Ruditis ★

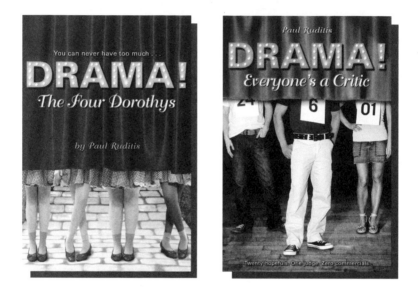

At Bryan Stark's posh private high school in Malibu, the teens are entitled, the boys are cute, and the school musicals are *extremely* elaborate. Bryan watches—and comments—as the action and intrigue unfold around him. Thrilling mysteries, comic relief, and epic sagas of friendship and love . . . It's all here. And it's showtime.

From Simon Pulse • Published by Simon & Schuster

Get smitten with these scrumptious British treats:

Prada Princesses
by Jasmine Oliver

Three friends tackle the high-stakes world of fashion school.

10 Ways to Cope with Boys
by Caroline Plaisted

What every girl *really* needs to know.

Does Snogging Count as Exercise?
by Helen Salter

For any girl who's tongue-tied around boys.

From Simon Pulse · Published by Simon & Schuster

Did you **love** this book?

Want to get the hottest books **free**?

Log on to
www.SimonSaysTEEN.com
to find out how you can get
free books from **Simon Pulse**
and become part of our **IT Board**,
where you can tell **US**, what **you** think!

SIMON
PULSE